I0609602

THE OYSTER SHELL DRIVEWAY

Douglas Atwill

THE OYSTER SHELL DRIVEWAY

A Novel

SUNSTONE
PRESS

SANTA FE

© 2013 by Douglas Atwill
All Rights Reserved.

No part of this book may be reproduced in any form or by any electronic or
mechanical means including information storage and retrieval systems
without permission in writing from the publisher, except by a reviewer
who may quote brief passages in a review.

Sunstone books may be purchased for educational, business, or sales promotional use.
For information please write: Special Markets Department, Sunstone Press,
P.O. Box 2321, Santa Fe, New Mexico 87504-2321.

Book design › Vicki Ahl
Body typeface › Poliphilus MT Pro
Printed on acid-free paper

Library of Congress Cataloging-in-Publication Data

Atwill, Douglas.
  The Oyster Shell driveway : a novel / by Douglas Atwill.
    pages cm
  ISBN 978-0-86534-928-5 (softcover : alk. paper)
  1. Novelists--Fiction. 2. Summer--California--Los Angeles--Fiction.
  3. Summer--California--Laguna Beach--Fiction. I. Title.
  PS3601.T85O97 2013
  813'.6--dc23

                            2013019644

WWW.SUNSTONEPRESS.COM
SUNSTONE PRESS / POST OFFICE BOX 2321 / SANTA FE, NM 87504-2321 /USA
(505) 988-4418 / ORDERS ONLY (800) 243-5644 / FAX (505) 988-1025

Preface

Changing the place of your life, moving on to convert your old problems into new ones, is often frowned upon by peers. We are taught to face up to disagreeable patches like good schoolboys, to stand our ground, to take the bad with the good. Common knowledge tells that the green pastures in the next county are mere illusions and only a fool pursues them. Mattox Williams, nonetheless, is choosing to move away to the West Coast, at least for long enough to finish his novel.

I often wonder if a summer, or a half year, on a small Greek island would help with my work at hand, whatever it happened to be. Would I return a changed man, a rearranged man, who has absorbed into his very being the good qualities and unimagined inspirations of a seaside sojourn? If I cannot in person make such change, I can certainly arrange for the narrator of this book to do exactly that. Mattox's everyday worries and concerns are left back at his house in Santa Fe as he takes on new experiences by the sea.

Just as I put a difficult painting face to the wall for a while or an unresolved story on the shelf, a time of differentness hones the eye and the ear like nothing else. To step back for a while may be one of the most creative steps we can take. Is it possible that, instead of a daydream villa on Patmos, I could rent the adjoining cottage, join my narrator for foggy mornings and a pounding Pacific surf? I wake up with a start and realize that my row of seaside cottages doesn't exist except in the pages of fiction.

Or does it?

—Douglas Atwill

1

Sparkling Diamonds

The leased piano arrived that morning and I asked the delivery men to place it against the inner wall of the living room, safely away, I thought, from the damaging sun of the east-facing windows. The flat side went all the way from one door to another, black and well-polished, a foreign authority in my house of pine tables and canvas-covered chairs. I remembered the teacher who told me that music hates the sun, that pianos needed to be at the back of stages or in gloomy parlors. Although it was well out of the damaging effects of the bright light, it seemed to exude an unease.

Olivia Montelle would take up her three month lease at noon. It was time to vacate the house, my one-bedroom with thick walls and casement windows. The climbing roses were in full bloom, *Cecile Brunner* in a buxom array and the rows of ripened Italian and French lettuces in the kitchen garden asked to be cut, brought in and tossed with a simple vinaigrette. Or, at least, they asked me with a clear voice; I wondered if Olivia would hear their green, rustling words or understand what they meant.

The weather was warm for May, so I had been propping open the French doors day and night, garden aromas filling the house. Cumulus clouds with dark undersides built up each morning over the mountains behind Santa Fe, a sure sign of early storms.

Why was I leaving this paradise in high season, the house in its walled garden, rows of white lilies in full bud, and the promise of afternoon showers? Was it so important to get away? Now that the time had come, these questions grew in stature, undermining my resolve.

Olivia had rented the house for the full summer. She was the high-visibility soprano for this season's opera, six performances of Tosca. My friends told me that she was the cream on top of the cream; you will find no better tenant. She's accustomed to fine things and will take care of your treasures. Olivia will move in and I must depart.

The rental was a notion, a solution, a way out of the status quo, during a morning a few weeks ago filled with self-pity and gloom. It would be a summer away from Santa Fe, a time to get back on track. I made the call to the rental director at the opera, a woman that I knew from music-centered dinner parties, and before I had time to think, I had a signed contract. An opera assistant in a well-tailored gray suit delivered the manila envelope with three months' rent in advance. The bridge was now in flames.

I was pulling the luggage together for my summer away: stacks of clothes, books, toiletries and other items necessary for a moveable life. Wilfred Cooper, a longtime friend and the one who might miss me the most, was helping me pack, amusing me while I sorted out the chaff. He sat on the brick sill of the bedroom casements, the morning sun streaming across him into the room. I folded clothes and packed them into the suitcases open on the bed. Shorts and light cotton shirts, denims, chinos, swimming trunks into the large case, books and writing paper all neatly fit into the medium one, and a duffel bag for everything else. What had I forgotten for a summer in California?

Wilfred, who was always chilly, wore a wool sweater on this warm day, and he leaned back against the windows, absorbing the nurture from the sun, his long legs crossed. He asked, "Where will you stay, Mattox?"

"I hoped somewhere by the sea." I folded the last tee shirt and started on the shorts.

"Could be chancey. The worst summer of my life was by the sea with Gerald. We took a clammy cottage on Block Island, arguments every day. The final straw was when Gerald berated me for slicing celery the wrong way, wrenching the knife right out of my hand. I caught the next ferry back."

"You've told me about that before. Maybe your time with Gerald was, in fact, over, celery or not."

"Of course, you're right. I'm too highly strung."

"Zoloft has helped you, I think."

Wilfred looked at me intently, considering the effect of his medication. "But are you sure that you will be all right?"

"I'll be okay. I can explore Pasadena and Laguna for the book, refresh my memories. Laura says that it needs a lot of work."

"You've heard from her finally?"

"She sent back the first draft."

"You didn't tell me. I gather from your tone that she savaged you?"

"She wrote on the title page:

> *Everyone in the book seems to live*
> *so much on the surface—I felt like*
> *I was in a Beckett play."*

"There are worse things than being in a Beckett play. Was she right?"

"Probably. I need slow mornings, stretches of white-space to think about the changes."

"You'll solve it. You always do," Wilfred said.

"Has she sold your book yet?" I asked, knowing he, too, had a manuscript doing the rounds.

"Five outright rejections. Not what the better firms were looking for, she said." Wilfred, after a long career as a painter, was a published writer. The memoir of his troubled youth in an upstate New York Quaker family, *Plowing in a Bonnet,* was well-received, earning good reviews and large sales, but the two volumes of light verse that followed earned a disappointing little. Yet he only found time to write now, the easel collecting dust. Writing is my life's work, he told me.

I followed his lead into writing, although not abandoning painting altogether. We shared the same New York literary agent, Laura Grabowski. Her actions or inactions often came up in our talks.

My first book, a collection of short stories, was published last fall: two dozen tales about the art colony in Santa Fe. The good reviews, on close inspection, fell into the category of faint praise, the critics awaiting the better efforts to come. One reviewer said that he looked forward to a longer piece, wherein the characters were not the merest of silhouettes. He asked where was the classic bohemian icon, the struggling artist?

My second book concerned a man, not too different from me, who recalled his years with a distinctive grandmother, while making sense out of life now as a mature painter and his love for a younger man. It was a novel set in the California of my youth, alternating with chapters about the Santa Fe of now. The narrator was me, and not me.

> *Laura: The structure is interesting,*
> *moving from first person to third,*
> *but I'm not sure why you've chosen it,*
> *as it actually makes the read somewhat confusing.*

Wilfred pulled a nail clipper out of his pocket, a wedge with a curved clipping blade, and while he snipped said, "Is it really to work on the book or are you just running away from Richard's death?"

He directed the nail clippings to land together on the window ledge.

"Both. I've been very restless, need a change." The largest suitcase was filled, so I pressed down with my knee, pulled the locks closed. The medium-sized case was next.

"You can't actually run away from it, you know, as you tried last winter. Like having an ugly nose or being too short. It's always there." Clip, clip, clip.

I said, "When I was young, there was no possibility to up and flee. Proper young men stayed and faced life. Take the caning with a brave heart, my son."

"I still have the marks on my bottom. Emotionally, anyway."

"We were the dutiful sons, Wilfred, young and callow. Now that I'm older, I know plenty of people who have successfully fled the unworkable, finding the sunny uplands."

"Like who?"

"Anne Lu; she packed her jewels and check books, sped off from two successive unsuitable husbands with the convertible top down, hair in the wind, mine-cut diamonds sparkling. She never looked back." Anne Lu was the mother of my first lover, a woman of style whose family money gave her the right to be willful, disagreeable and slippery in commitments.

"Did that make her happy?" Wilfred asked.

"She did not know how to be happy, but it took her away from the prime source of irritation. She moved on."

"Who else?"

"That jeweler on Galisteo Street, I forget his name. He made millions on gold rings and emerald brooches, but never paid a penny to the IRS. A premonition one night told him to sell up. He did, well below market value, paid the employees their hush money and fled into the West Indies. Still there, still tan and happy, for all I know."

"Both very colorful, but you can't just walk away. The memory of Richard's death will follow you." Wilfred's emery board smoothed the ragged edges of the newly cut nails, while the foot on his crossed leg pumped up and down as if keeping time to music.

"I am going to run away, nevertheless."

"Will you take a photograph of him with you?"

"Of course. This one right here. I don't expect to forget him, only to have some ease, to sleep at night." It was a color picture of Richard, in tee-shirt and shorts with a hand on the collar of his dog, a black standard poodle named Jameson. Richard looked happy in the snapshot, a condition not always so in his short life.

"Mattox, you should find somebody new to love. Join the hunt like the rest of us. Smokey nights in pick-up bars, waking up on ill-sheeted beds."

"We'll see. Bars were never my best act."

"Well then, drive carefully across the desert. Call me." Wilfred uncrossed his legs, stood up and brushed the nail clippings into a pile before dropping them into the waste-basket.

I asked him, "By the way, what is the right way to slice celery?"

"On the diagonal, Gerald said. The long cut enhances the flavor, as every good Japanese chef knows."

He hugged me, and quickly stepped out of the door without looking back.

In two minutes, he walked back up the brick path with Olivia Montelle on his arm. I saw them chatting and laughing, Wilfred's charm light at full wattage. As I opened the front door, he said, "Hello, again. I met this exotic creature in your driveway. It was only polite to deliver her safely to her new home."

A kaftan covered Olivia's height with an African pattern of black and white zig-zags, her black eyes and matte-black ringlets matching. I wondered if she wore a wig taken from the opera stores, covering mousey hair in a thin military cut underneath. I had seen her only once before, through binoculars ten rows from stage. A head taller than most women, she dwarfed the tenors she was often paired with. She had a voice that rattled the entry doors. Was she too old for Tosca?

Wilfred took her arm as she stepped up the tall front step to my house. She said, "Mr. Williams, I can't tell you how excited I am about a summer in this house. I read about it last winter in the coffee-table book of Santa Fe houses, studied every room. I had no idea it would ever be available for lease. How can you give it up?"

"I didn't think about actually leaving until this morning. The sun woke me up early and as I lay there I asked myself, what have I done?"

"You're not going to renege, are you?" She put a hand up to her cheek in a theatrical gesture of worry. Perhaps all gestures had become theatrical for Olivia.

"Don't worry. I'm actually looking forward to California, much as I'll miss Ben and the garden." The Bengal cat, Ben, heard his name spoken and responded with a series of meows. The imposing form of Olivia gave him a start, so he slid back in silence under the sofa. The rental office said that she was a cat person and had agreed to care for him in the contract.

"All cats love me," she said. "He'll take to me once he comes out. I'll see to it that he has a good summer. May I cook little treats for him, like chopped liver canapés and fish-balls with shrimp sauce?"

"He would be delighted. Dry pellets poured straight from the box are what Ben gets from me." He gave more loud meows from floor level.

"Now, I will test the Steinway." There was something too-perfect in her diction, her pronunciation; maybe from years of tutoring to mask an East Texas girlhood. I waved her into the living room where the long black instrument hugged the inside wall, an uneasy Visigoth on his first day in Rome.

She said, "It wants to be away from the wall so people can walk freely around it. Music cannot be crowded. At dinners for my opera friends, they will encircle the piano making song, gesticulating all the while. We can't have their hands banging against your beautiful walls. I've already called the piano man to tune it this afternoon."

The piano was on casters, so the three of us rolled it on the tumbled-brick floor away from the constricting wall and deeper into the room. It made high, jingling sounds with twangs from the bass strings. She lifted the lid over the keyboard and ruffled a scale while she stood and winced.

"I've read that pianos in our altitude almost race out of tune." Wilfred said. "They need adjusting every two months or so, harpsichords and clavichords even more often."

"Seven thousand feet is hard on the voice as well," she said. "Mr. Williams…"

"Please, just Mattox."

"Mattox, then, how will you fill your days in California? Sunning and relaxing?"

Wilfred answered, "He's promised his literary agent to finish his novel, to explore boyhood haunts. Most of Santa Fe knows him as a painter, but at this late date in his career he's taken up writing. What's the world coming to, painters turning into writers, stay-at-homes turning into runaways?"

"I have the notion that nobody's happy with their talents," I answered. "Down deep, painters want to write, writers want to paint, and dancers want to sing. At some point people want a change, to spread their wings a bit."

"I'll only want to sing," Olivia said, looking pointedly at me. "However, I would be immeasurably happier singing if I lived in a house like this. What is your novel about?"

"Growing up in California with a grandmother and her impossible love for a foreigner. My writer friends say you risk bad luck to describe a manuscript any more than that."

"Impossible loves. I've had some of those," she said.

"They are the difficult ones that you remember."

Olivia said, "I'm sorry you're leaving. I think we could be good friends." She looked at me with sharp eyes, assessing the possibility of friend-like qualities lying barely beneath my exterior.

With his face out of Olivia's view, Wilfred did an eye roll and excused himself, hugging me again. "I'll just leave you with your new friend." He turned around on the path and waved as he departed.

Giving Olivia a card, I said, "Here is my cell phone number in case something goes wrong or Ben is off his feed. If I'm going to make the Grand Canyon by dark, I need to leave now."

"Don't worry anymore, everything will be fine. See, your Ben is out and on his cushion. We're already beginning to bond." She flashed a white-toothed stage smile that surely could have been seen from the balcony's back row. It did little to allay my misgivings. The first rumble of thunder came from the mountain clouds, storms now higher and closer.

2

Cool Water, No Sharks

All my suitcases, the lap-top computer, the printer, six reams of copy paper and two dozen books, including my annotated first draft, fit into the car's luggage compartment by pressing down hard on the lid. I closed the windows and locked the front door of my separate studio building, an old adobe with Greek revival trim, tall windows with wavy glass and brick floors. The studio was not included in Olivia's lease. I would miss the hours I spent each morning in front of the easel.

With rain coming, I left the convertible top closed. I drove down Old Pecos Trail to the interstate highway just as the storm came crashing upon me: hail, rain and lightning. Rivulets coursed down my windshield, and I decided that showers so early in the season were the good omen I was looking for, a sign for a good trip. Wasn't there a New England platitude about leaving harbor in a storm, returning on a fair breeze?

I did not tell Olivia the real reason for my trip to the coast: a release from the burning picture in my mind of Richard's dead body on the Barbados beach. Each time I glanced at his Buddhism books on the shelf, his clothes folded in a drawer, or the crabapple he planted in the vegetable garden, a fixed image came up of his gray body on the beach, waves washing his feet. It was the same spot where on the day before we had collected pieces of brain coral, where sea-grape trees angled out over the water-edge to make a pool of shade. The rescuers had pulled him in there, just another drowning victim to them. How does an experienced swimmer drown in a calm sea? How does a veteran climber fall from a mountain? Life is fragile.

In the months that followed painting proved impossible. I tried to hide in front of the easel, starting again and again the paintings for the gallery that sold my canvases. My mind wandered, the act of mixing paint and applying it too natural to block out thought. Having too much spare time to ponder, the brain resurrected that branded picture that I wanted to forget.

When I turned from painting and started to write each morning, it was a liberation. My mind became more fully occupied, that waterside drama crowded out by words, phrases and the crafting of sentences. How much of the world's writing was propelled forward by this avoidance, the author hiding from intrusive memories, shutting grief away while the mind grappled with words? I thought about Olivia's out-of-tune piano with sympathy; perhaps I was out-of-tune as well, needing an expert tightening of the strings to get back on track.

I long ago learned to flick my eyes to the right, then to the left, to stop the pictures in my mind. It was a trick my alcoholic sister-in-law taught me, a technique they gave her in the rehabilitation clinics. Flick right, flick left, two or three repetitions and the image was erased.

As I drove south towards Albuquerque, the scattered storms alternated with brief interludes of sun. The freeway through the city was dark and wet. An hour west, the rolling scrub land gave way to red-rocked cliffs in the distance. The storms began to thin and I felt an excitement welling about the summer, a renewal about to happen. Guilt started to dissolve like a breeze clearing away the smog of a city. California, the classic destination for new awakenings and re-discovery, awaited. Generations had found a new life there, so why wouldn't I?

Approaching the Arizona border, the cliffs of Navajo country came closer to the road like shy animals now emboldened, their sienna red haunches marbleized with long strata of linen white, smoothed by centuries of weather. The dark green speckling of piñon and juniper balanced the red walls of the escarpments, suggesting Cezanne's comment that every landscape painting was a battle between red and green. A truth from a man who had never been to this Navajo country, where bloody clay-red fought every day with the dark Jenkins Green of the conifers, every shade struggling with its opposite. He would smile if he saw how apt his remark was.

Across into eastern Arizona, the land slowly revealed its secrets, one geology lesson after another. A meterorite crater, the petrified forest, a painted desert, lava fields and finally, the dormant volcano itself, guarding the access to the canyon.

The sun slid below view as I drove up to the old hotel, the sky full of clouds washed with the cadmium colors: red, orange, deep yellow. The hotel was a large, log building stained deep brown: pinon-smoke from winter fires lurked in the lobby, the incensed aroma absorbed by the walls themselves.

"You're a lucky man, you are. We've been fully booked all day, but a cancellation popped up on my screen just as you walked up. The Bright Angel Suite." The young clerk signed me in, wide-eyed with his computer expertise, claiming no other room was available at a lower price. No discounts were possible, sir. No, not even AAA.

As he handed me the key, he said, "It's good to see an American at the canyon, sir. We get so many Japanese and Germans at this time of year."

I took all the luggage up to the suite, where turquoise-painted French doors gave out onto a terrace overlooking the entire panorama of the canyon. It was obvious why they gave no discounts for the Bright Angel Suite; on the terrace I sat as the colors faded from full strength to rosy violet to pale blue. When it was nearly dark, the glimpse of Venus almost touching a crescent moon peeked through the clouds. Was Islam nearby?

I must not let myself think about Richard. The Pacific coast loomed larger in my mind, with its cool waters and compelling sunsets. I would force myself further back in time, to my Laguna summers, the happy, high voices of boyhood calling above the crash of the surf. The smell of suntan oils and salty beaches. If the novel was nothing more than a first effort, clumsy and replete with errors as Laura implied, it could be fixed, improved, enriched. Ninety days of summer, four pages a day. All was possible as I sat on the terrace, stars and moon giving me strength.

Opening my cell-phone cover to see if there was a signal, I called Bob Dermott in Palm Springs, a half-day's drive away.

"Bob, I'm at the Grand Canyon, finally on my way. I'll get an early start and be there just after lunch."

"Great. Guest room sheets are washed, tables dusted and scorpions on the run. We await the prodigal son."

"Let me take you to dinner, if you aren't already spoken for."

"I'll book an eight o'clock table at Davey's right now. You know how busy they can be."

"Even in summer?"

"There are a lot of us here in the valley now, all year round."

The next day I was on the road while the sun was still low behind me. The crowded ponderosa pines in the road-side forests gave way to the smaller piñons as I drove west. Down in altitude, stands of sturdy junipers took over, the edge-of-the-desert evergreens, scrappy survivors in the dry foothills.

Eventually, even the junipers thinned out and ocotillos began, long Old Testament branches of thorns with the red flowers now dried in the growing summer heat. I put down the convertible top and lowered speed across the warming desert; I savored the idea of arriving in Palm Springs in an open car, now shiny clean from the rains. Maybe black was not a foolish color after all.

Bob lived in a condominium near the Movie Colony, a collection of stucco and red-tiled villas around an Olympic-sized swimming pool, palm trees, olive trees, oranges in fragrant bloom and lawns so green that they hurt the eyes. The perimeter wall with coded gates kept out the unworthy. Bob told me that the citrus trees were shorn of fruit by the gardeners before they ripened lest rats came to dine at night on the pink grapefruit or tangerines. It was sad and non-productive, no free meals for *Rattus Rattus Rattus* in this Eden. Picking and eating citrus directly from the tree had always been a secret vice for me, an illicit pleasure you must not confess to those in authority.

After I settled into Bob's guest room, I put on swimming trunks and walked to the pool, which I had to myself. The heat was an intense, pounding wall as I slid into the water. Thirty laps in the pool refreshed me, but the sun was still fierce. Bob came out to join me on the last laps, sitting and watching on the pool's edge with his legs in the water.

He had the elongated good looks of his small-eyed Nordic forebears. Barely older than the last time I saw him, his movements were more studied, the bending down to poolside slower than before. There was no change, however, in his perfect tan complexion and expertly cut, abundant white hair, style being important, maybe even more so as the years mounted.

He said, "Stay here for a while. Nobody's used the guest room for weeks."

"I thought about renting a cottage on the coast."

"Stay here; this is the best water-side cottage in Southern California. Good restaurants, friendly natives, cool water, no sharks."

I said, "It's too hot for me here, Bob. I know that fog and cool mornings will help me write, pamper me. What about Santa Barbara? You have friends there, don't you?"

"I do, but they are all very rich. The likes of us can't afford even the smallest apartment, blocks away from the beach."

"What about north of there?"

"There is a small beach town before Morro Bay called Glitter Bay. I went through it years ago. I've heard it's not expensive."

"I'll look there. It would be only a couple of hours drive back to Pasadena or Laguna."

"Why Pasadena?"

I pulled myself out of the water and we retreated to the chairs in the shade of an umbrella. "The book. It's about growing up in Pasadena and I need to refresh the images, look at old neighborhoods, get things right."

"And Laguna?"

"I used to stay there with my grandmother. She had a cottage on

Waterbird Lane, and that name and the foggy mornings are about all that I remember of it."

"I'll call my friend Dom Histriodes in Laguna and tell him you might come by. He has a bistro on the Coast Highway there. You'll like him and he has a guest house."

"I would rather stay in a hotel."

"I understand. I'll call him, anyway."

"Thanks."

3

Nirvana

We were on time for the reservation at Davey's, Bob claiming that the owners gave away the tables for late arrivals. The main room, almost full with middle-aged and older men, occasionally accompanied by buffed, younger companions, was encircled with booths, larger tables spread across the center. The conversations made the room noisy. The owner seated us at the one remaining empty booth, green leather cushions and an overhanging light.

After we had ordered medium rare steaks with no potatoes, green salads with dressing on the side, Bob said, "Excuse me for a moment. I see some dear friends that I have to talk to." He walked over to a far booth and stood talking to a white-haired foursome.

The room was full of men enjoying being with their own kind. How comfortable Palm Springs was, gay bars, gay restaurants and entire gay neighborhoods. For a small city, it was a haven of tolerance. I thought of Eleanor, my old Santa Fe neighbor and shopkeeper, convinced that summer Bible students from Glorieta shop-lifted her small items, put a sign on the screen door: *No Baptists*. Palm Springs did not need to erect a *No Bigots* sign, because the judgmental knew better than to tarry there.

As I was looking around the room, a wide-shouldered man with a small waist, certainly a body builder, came up to the table and said, "You are beautiful." He had perfect teeth as he smiled.

Caught by total surprise, I pulled enough wits together to say, "Sit down, let's talk." He moved into the seat opposite me with cat-like ease. His face was broad and square, hair cut short like a military man.

"Is that your lover over there?" he asked. His voice was as deep as a basso, the silver-haired Commenditore.

"No, a good friend. I'm staying tonight in his guest room. A one night visit."

"Lucky man." I thought with amusement of this reversal. It was customarily me who walked up to the table of a younger man, charming him, inviting him. In this paradise for older men, I had become the prey.

"Do you live in Palm Springs?" I asked.

"Four years now."

"Life seems good here."

"It is. Can you come home with me after dinner, without your good friend?"

"No, thanks. What part of town do you live in?"

"Nirvana for you, but most people call it Deep Well Ranch."

"Where did you learn to smooth-talk like that?"

"It comes naturally when I want something. Why don't you stay a while longer? Only a few days. I will make love to you and we could get acquainted." He reached across the pool of light and put his two hands over mine. They were warm, tanned, curiously smooth for being so large. It was an agreeable change to be wanted, to be touched in anticipation again, a small electrical charge that was missing in everyday contact. I wondered if I should accept his offer.

"I'm going to Glitter Bay, a working summer finishing my novel," I said. " I'll be back through in September."

"Here's my card, Mr. Glitter Bay. My name's Axton. Call when you come here again. You can slowly read to me what you have written, while I stroke your chest, fondle your brow, make you crazy with desire."

"How could I say no?" As he stood up to leave, he leaned down, put a hand behind my head and firmly pulled me into his kiss. It was short and he tasted slightly of Martini; afterwards, he smiled directly at me.

Bob, as well as the four men he went to meet, had all turned their heads my way as Axton returned to his own booth behind me. If Palm

Springs was the fabled sophisticated retreat from Los Angeles, curiosity lived here as in any small town. I did a thumbs-up to the group. What Axton would have said if I had replied that Bob was my lover? Much the same, I thought.

Bob returned and sat down. "It didn't take you long to feel right at home. My friends were impressed."

"I didn't summon him up, he just came over. Do you know him? His name is Axton."

"We see him at the gym, but he never gave any of us a welcome like that. They say that he was an Air Force colonel, a jet bomber pilot and a marine before that. He lives on a double military pension. Double-chromosomes, as well, from the look of it." So he was Don Giovanni's father-in-law, winged helmet and all.

"I'm not really in the market."

"Nonsense. We're always in the market."

That night as I turned out the light in Bob's guest room, nestled down in the air-conditioned comfort, it felt good to be noticed again, to be sought out. My sensual part for so long had been turned down low, and now I could feel the first bubbles of steam. How different California was from my small Santa Fe. People here say right away what they want, make advances and live in the world of today. I was accustomed to the reticence of my own circle of friends, so what would this letting-the-fences-down mean for me? Did a new life really await?

4

Kamikaze Bar

Bob did not believe in a hearty breakfast. A glass of grapefruit juice and a single cup of Irish Breakfast Tea were part of what kept him slim, and each he offered to me.

"I do have some instant coffee somewhere back there on that shelf." he said, when he studied my expression of disappointment.

"I'll find it. Caffeine, however it arrives, is a must for me."

"Tea has caffeine."

"Too English and too weak."

I boiled the water while he spread his well-folded map of Southern California on the breakfast table. Glitter Bay was at least a three-hour drive to the northwest. We traced the route from Palm Springs to avoid the freeways, through Victorville, Boron, Mojave, south of Bakersfield, Maricopa, through the oil fields of Cuyama to Santa Maria and finally over the remnants of the Coast Range to the sea. It was all on the smaller back roads, a journey so many had taken to California. Anything was possible on the Pacific Coast, a mantra written into the very bones of Americans. When nothing worked in your home town, a trip west could kick start a whole new life.

These were the back roads leading through small towns with court-house squares unchanged from the 1920s. The wide concrete streets planted with double rows of the Canary Island palms, now sought out by horticultural bounty hunters, large tree machines taking them up and replanting them on esplanades in Laguna Niguel farther south. Soon there would be no majesty in these Valley towns, first shorn of their water-rights and now of these last vestiges of dignity.

After Santa Maria I would head over to the Coast Highway One, where the names took on the utopian excitement of early California: Oceano, Halcyon and finally, Glitter Bay, on the map in very small type-face, just under the larger type of Morro Bay. I thought of Richard's belief in omens, when a wind knocked an object off a table or a book fell to the floor when I bumped into the shelves. Pay attention, he said, it might be a message from another place. On the map, Glitter Bay seemed to be saying notice me, notice me, glittering. I will pay attention, Richard, I promise.

Bob said, "Watch out, these back roads are poorly marked. You'll grow tired of a backwater like Glitter Bay, I know, so plan to come here any weekend that you can't stand it anymore."

"Thanks. I have a picture of the perfect cottage waiting for me. A shingled affair opening out onto a seaside terrace, a view of the breakers where I can write wearing a sweater each morning as the fog lifts. It will be only a short walk to a good swimming beach, simple cafes with *lattes* and *cappucinos* waiting on the first inland street, English and French newspapers in the racks."

"You've seen too much *Wizard of Oz*. Truth is, it's what everybody else in California wants. A forgotten town, low real estate prices, sophisticated aura."

"I'm sure it awaits."

He said, "You'll have to drive down to Santa Barbara for a gay bar with a friendly face."

"I've never been a bar person. If I get desperate, I'll call Axton."

The trip took five hours on the two-lane roads, the last stretch in tight curves over the green hills and live oak groves of the Coast Range, still verdant from winter rains. A few small wineries with newly planted vines dotted the ranch pastures. The vineyards had names like Serendipity Hills and Merlin's Reach, the young vines sporting a dozen green leaves each in long rows. All hope and promise.

Glitter Bay itself was a single paved street parallel to the coast highway, dotted with beach businesses, vacation motels, dive shops, bed and breakfasts, three cafes and one bar, the Kamikaze. Leggy geraniums grew without care as big as small trees. The ocean access from the single main street was a series of gravel side streets with shingled cottages and picket fences, heading west across the dunes.

The clerk at the Lone Palm Motel was a middle-aged woman with deep red hair working intently on her long, square-ended artificial nails. Was the whole world clipping their nails? Without looking up at me, she asked whether I wanted a room with a kitchenette for eighty dollars a day or a standard double for fifty. Buff, buff, polish, polish.

"The standard. Is there a weekly rate and a Triple-A discount?" I said. There were both, she said, so I booked for a week. She entered the information into the motel computer with the eraser end of a pencil, slowly, one key after the other, her nails too ornamental for everyday tasks.

"Do you know of cottages to rent for the summer?" I asked. "Perhaps along the beach?"

"Everyone wants to be out there. They are probably already all rented, but you can ask at the rental agent two doors down." She pointed with the pencil behind her towards the north; it was clear that she did not care very much about my search.

I drove around to park in front of my room, which had a chenille-spreaded bed, black-and-white television and one chair, no writing table. Not much cheer, either. With some luck I would be out of there in less than a week.

I unloaded the three suitcases and the laptop. My head was still full of the images of the drive through the expiring center of California, and I wanted to get them written before their sharpness softened. This was the California of my boyhood, now a bit mummified, but features intact.

Piling the bed pillows and the rolled-up chenille spread into a back-rest, I got to work as the afternoon grew into early evening. Three pages of description of what things looked like in central California: the farm trucks heavy with crates of artichokes, asparagus and early tomatoes; shuttered mom-and-pop grocery stores with the family names of California immigrants: Tonobedian Market, Yamaguchi Produce, Chang's Store, Petrillo Family Market, Verdi and Brother Market; abandoned juice stands, orange-painted globes with a single, shuttered window (*Do you want crushed ice in your juice, young man?*); the green abundance of high grass and wildflowers around even the smallest houses, summer's heat still to come; single overgrown citrus trees in backyards; many-branched pomegranate trees with green, unripe globes; avocado trees encircled with a dark ring of fallen fruit; a sign in one town for Korean Massage with Green Tara Lotion; a flock of emus running their strange gait through the hill pastures like cattle; the bank of fog roiling above the coast range, hiding Shangri-la on its other side.

It was about seven o'clock when, too late for a visit to the house-rental agent, I went down to the Kamikaze Bar for a drink or two before dinner. A fake Zero airplane crashed at an angle into the roof with a smiling dummy in the pilot seat.

Inside, the bar was smoky, packed, and noisy with music and talk. A local decorator had followed through with the Japanese theme, red-circled flags stapled to the ceiling, leather aviator helmets and goggles hanging around on the walls, chairs and stools worked up from bamboo. Signs around the walls depicted Japanese clichés in large letters: "Ah, So," "Ohio!" "Flied Lice," and "Anne of Gleen Gables."

Where had so many people come from for Happy Hour? I took the stool that was vacant at the end of the bar. There was a friendly atmosphere, a California version of the Irish pub where locals gathered to talk and be seen. Everyone seemed to know everyone else. Equally spaced along the bar were three identical brass lamps in the shape of Hawaiian girls, hands behind their heads, hula skirts slowly undulating.

As I sat down, the woman who was behind the bar caught my eye and indicated she would come to me in a minute. When she did get around to me, I ordered a scotch and soda, with a lemon twist. She was harried, rushing back to her station at the other end to open beers and pour single shots with dexterity. It was clear that the Kamikaze was an after-five meeting place for working men, some in tan uniforms, others in denim jeans and shirts, and a few women similarly dressed. I could not read the emblem that was embroidered on their shirt pockets, but it seemed to be the same lightning-bolt design for all of them. I sipped my drink slowly.

The man next to me nodded and said hello. I replied, "A busy bar. Where does everybody work here?"

"The power station up at Morro Bay. This is the day shift coming home. In an hour, it will be just about empty. After work, we unwind."

By the time I had finished my second drink, the bar cleared out noticeably. The woman behind the bar relaxed after the crush and came over to talk. Her body was slim with small breasts, dark glasses turned up in her short blonde hair, and a deep tan. She was dressed in designer jeans that hugged her thin hips and a black silk blouse. If she were walking along the street, you would notice her.

"Where you from?" she asked.

"Santa Fe."

"New Mexico? I've been there; it's a lot different than Glitter Bay. Just passing through?"

"No, I was hoping to find a beach cottage here, to rent for the summer."

"The ones on the beach stay rented all year-round now. You on vacation?" She pulled up a stool behind the bar and sat down, opening a bottled Coke which she slowly poured into a glass with ice.

"No, I'm a writer, looking for a quiet place to finish a novel."

"We mostly get families here. Not many writers. It's a quiet place here."

"I thought a house on the beach would be perfect. I could walk for exercise along the beach, write most of the day, maybe even swim when it gets warmer, come here in the evening."

"It never gets warmer here. Turns you blue, even in August."

I said, "Do you know of cottages for rent or someone I could talk to?"

"No. You married?"

"I'm gay."

"You don't look gay."

"We come in all sizes, just like everybody else."

She drank up the rest of her coke and said, "Anyway, you should go back down to Santa Barbara. They have a lot of gay bars there. Or up to Carmel, it's full of artists."

"Thanks, but I'm not looking for bar action right now. Just a place off the beaten path to write."

"Well, you are off the beaten path." She excused herself to attend to some more orders at the other end of the bar. I finished up my glass with a rattle from the ice cubes and stood up to leave.

She motioned for me to sit down while she finished washing glasses at the sink, plunging them up and down on an underwater brush. Drying her hands on a towel, she came to my end again and said, "My name is Sylvan Pagano. I just thought of something. Maybe my brother, Hayden, would rent you a room."

"Does he have a house on the beach?"

"The best beach, Glitter Bay itself. A real classic cottage. Garnet Hardwick owns all the rest of the cottages there, but she sold one to Hayden a few years back. It has a couple of nice big bedrooms, separate bathrooms with their own baths."

"Maybe that could work out."

"Hayden's not gay, of course, but he can always use some extra money. He's at work at the power plant all day, so he wouldn't be in the way for your writing. Week-ends, he sometimes works at the Dive Shop. Hayden lives alone, since he can't keep a girl friend."

"Sounds perfect. Can I talk to him?"

"I'll call you tonight and let you know what he says. Where you staying?"

I told her and left the Kamikaze Bar. After an uninspired dinner at one of the cafés, I got into bed early at the motel. I was tired from the drive and dozed off while watching television, one rerun sitcom after another. The phone woke me. Sylvan said that Hayden first wants to meet you before deciding. Tomorrow is Saturday, so he'll be at the cottage. Come by the bar at eleven and you can follow me down there.

5

Mr. Fixit

I trailed after Sylvan's pick-up truck down Castle Drive to an unnamed side road, then straight out past cottages on either side to the sand dunes that separated the town from the beach. The gravel ended before the dunes, turning into a private driveway with a layer of crushed oyster shells that crunched under our wheels, a sharp sound.

On the beach side of the dunes the drive forked, giving separate access to each of the cottages facing the ocean. Sylvan drove north to the last cottage, the only one with a grove of banana trees in the side yard, full-grown trees twice the height of the cottage. A two-door red Jeep Cherokee was parked behind the cottage.

Sylvan and I walked along a path beside the banana trees around to the beach entrance, one of three pairs of French doors opening onto a sand-dusted brick terrace across the entire front of the house. The white paint on the doors needed repainting soon, the shingles on the walls turned a deep black-gray. She opened the door and I followed her inside.

There was none of the disorder I would have expected in the house of a single man. Sylvan called out for Hayden and walked to a back room as I looked around. The living room was sparsely furnished with an old tan leather sofa, two adjoining upholstered chairs. There was a thread-bare Bukhara rug on the floor, and, next to the other set of French doors, a dining table made from a hollow-core wood door, canvas backed director's chairs surrounding it. The ceiling beams were unpainted wood, with matching decking between. A kitchen opened into this room with an island and a row of bamboo bar stools, the same design as the Kamikaze Bar. A gift from Sylvan, perhaps.

The two of them walked out of the bedroom and Sylvan said, "This is Mattox Williams."

We shook hands and Hayden sat on one of the barstools. He was tall, broad-framed, light curly hair in abundance, about thirty-five years old, wearing faded denim shorts, a white tee-shirt and scuffed brown-leather loafers without socks. I noticed that we were the same height, although Hayden was wider at the shoulders, more fit, definitely younger, stronger.

Hayden said, "Sylvan says that you are a writer."

"A new writer. A book of stories came out this spring and I'm working on a novel. What do you do?" I never liked talking about myself for very long.

"I work at the power plant, an Engineer's Assistant."

Sylvan said, "That's a fancy term for a Mr. Fixit."

Hayden said, "I am good a fixing things, not a real engineer. Believe me, there's a lot of things at the plant that need looking after."

"I get nervous thinking that things need fixing at a nuclear plant."

"It's mostly the offices and store-rooms. Windows, doors, shelves, and the like. The containment building is off-limits to most of us."

"That makes me feel better. May I see the room I would rent?"

Hayden opened the door to the main bedroom, a large space with the third pair of French doors giving out onto the terrace. Clearly this was the master bedroom of the cottage, a full view of the ocean with an adjoining bathroom, complete with a tub, toilet and sink in the same pale green. The bedroom and bath were very close to what I foresaw in my morning departure from Bob Dermott's. Omens worked once again.

He said, "I will clear my stuff out of here, move to the back bedroom."

"I'll need a writing table, otherwise it's great. If you don't have one, I am sure I can buy one in town."

"No problem. I have another one the same size as the dining table."

I said, "You are lucky to own this cottage. I'll bet everybody wants to buy it from you."

"Every month or so I get an offer, but I won't sell. Garnet let me buy it three years ago, after I rented for five years. She asked me to never sell it."

Sylvan said, "She owns the whole beach, except for this one."

"Lucky woman."

She said, "Nothing lucky about it. She bought them years ago, one at a time, when nobody wanted to live out here because of the nuclear plant. They went for less than ten thousand each. Everybody wanted to sell, to get away. Crafty Garnet bought them all. We don't hear so much flack now about radiation from the plant."

Hayden said, "She lives in the cottage at the far end, and rents all the others out. She was a script girl for silent movies, saved her money, bought real estate."

I asked, "How old is Garnet?"

"Nobody really knows."

Although not apparent to me, it must have been plain to Sylvan that the process for my approval was nearly complete, because she said, "Hayden told me that the rent is a thousand a month, in advance. No deposit. You can share the kitchen and the front room."

I said, "That's fine. May I have it for the summer, then? Three months."

Hayden said, "It's yours. I'll move out this morning and you can move in later today, if that's what you want."

"I'll give you a check right now. This is perfect. I make it out to Hayden Pagano?"

Sylvan interrupted, "Pagano is my married name, divorced now. Our family name is Danning. He's Hayden Danning."

As I wrote out the check I could feel him watching my face intently, not the moving hand. He said, "I've never met a writer before. What is your book about?"

"Short stories about painters living in Santa Fe. I've been a painter there for twenty years, so it's a subject I know. I'll give you a copy."

"So you're an artist?"

"I'm taking some time off from the studio to write the next draft of a novel. Same theme again, a Santa Fe painter, this time with a back story of how he grew up like me in his grandmother's California house."

"Where did you and your grandmother live?"

"Pasadena and Laguna. I need to spend a few days in each of those places, to refresh memories. It should be an easy drive."

He said, "If you don't hit rush hour, you could go down and come back in the same day."

Sylvan said, "Our uncle teaches English at the junior college; he'll want to meet a real writer."

Hayden came over and shook my hand again, holding it together with his other hand. I felt his animal energy like a bolt, a physical warmth that spread up my arm and throughout my body. It was a strong sexual energy. He must have seen my response, because he smiled and put his hand on my shoulder, which only increased the tingling intensity elsewhere. He folded the check and put it in his pocket.

Would it be possible to get work done with such a sensual generator in the next room? A summer in the front room of Mr. Fixit could be a lot more interesting that I had counted upon.

6

Crushed Black Beetles

I drove back into town and chose another of the three cafes for breakfast. There was a vacant stool at the counter. I already felt that I belonged in this seaside community, a townie, as I ordered eggs over-easy and a side of crisp bacon.

Back at the Lone Palm Motel, the desk clerk at first refused to refund my payment for the days not used, claiming the owners did not repay discounted rents, it was a firm policy. When I told her that I was moving over to Hayden Danning's for the summer, her refusal dissolved. Glitter Bay took care of its own. She had switched from fingernails to toenails. I packed up and drove out to the beach.

The French doors to the front bedroom opened easily, a surprise in this salt-spray setting. I remembered the difficult doors at my grandmother's house in Laguna, often wedged so tightly shut that I had to use my shoulders to force them open, once breaking several panes of glass in the process. No doubt Hayden, handy with a wood-plane and an Allen wrench, spent time on his own windows and doors. He had already cleared out his belongings from the room, the closet and drawers empty of clothes, bathroom cleaned.

I set up the lap-top computer on the table by the doors, stacked the books in piles on the far side and plugged in the printer. Both lap-top and printer worked perfectly. Then I arranged the clothes in the dresser drawers and on hangers in the closet. A look into the living room revealed that Hayden was in the back bedroom, no sound issuing from there. Eager to walk on the beach again, I changed into shorts and tee shirt, took my shoes off.

The firmly packed sand right next to the water was flat and easy to walk on. The surf was relaxed, not the prize-winning rollers of my youth. I went south past the other cottages with no outward evidence of occupants in any of them. Two of the cottages had sea-pines growing nearby and all had clusters of century plants, giant and blue-green beside the surf, and the ever-present ice-plant that spread where traffic did not wear it down.

Hayden must have added the French doors and brick terrace to his own cottage, because none of the others had more than a flat stretch of sand on the seafront, sliding glass doors and wooden Adirondack chairs. A smaller clutch of banana trees also grew at the last cottage, a sign lettered with Hardwick over the doors, and it had a terrace of old brick in basket-weave. Hayden was responsible for these improvements, I was sure, a project to favor his benefactoress.

The sun had not burned away the vestiges of the morning fog. I walked around the narrow promontory at the south end and onto the beach of the next cove, a long crescent completely devoid of buildings or any sign of the works of man. The ice-plants covering on the dunes were in full magenta bloom, a chemical color in this otherwise unfettered scene, as if the I.G.Farben company had invented a groundcover.

The sounds and aromas of the beach brought up memories of boyhood, the worries and joys of an uneasy aesthete, unlike his schoolmates in many ways. I remembered the bonfires along the beach on the nights of grunion runs, shallow waters thick with laughing families trying to catch with their hands the slippery females, anxious to slip by the predators and deposit their eggs in high-water sand. The local papers ran a small notice on full moon nights:

The grunion are running tonight on Laguna beaches
after 9:14. Remember, it is against
California law for citizens
to catch grunion with anything but their hands.

Does the mature mind remember only the more festive times, the feast days and the funerals, forgetting the long days of sameness, inaction? I strongly recalled the grunion nights on the beach as my cousins and I cooked the small fish over the bonfires. The sardine-like catch was unceremoniously pierced onto sticks, roasting them until they sizzled.

I walked knee-deep out into the waters of the cove beyond Garnet's house, and it was as cold as Sylvan claimed. Perhaps, with some firm resolve, I could try a swim in a month or two, as the midsummer ocean arrived at its zenith.

When I first learned to swim in Laguna, my grandmother's neighbors grumbled about the low temperature of the water, claiming the Humboldt Current had come closer to shore making the sea-water much colder than the halcyon years of their own childhoods. There were various man-caused reasons for this. It was the dratted automobiles, they said, destroying the citrus orchards with their fumes and now Mother Nature was punishing us for not respecting the land. Over-development. Radio waves. Godlessness. We all must pray harder, because Satan was afoot. Cold waters preceded the Apocalypse.

So I was at last was back in California, the childhood home I had abandoned, a place in my mind of bright sun, long shadows, earthquakes that turned the wood-framed rooms into unstable parallelograms, tidal waves that crashed without warning over jetty light-houses, wild-fires in the hills and winter storms with winds so strong that the hundred-foot eucalyptus trees fell onto slow-moving automobiles, crushing the occupants like so many black beetles.

Did I really walk to school over sidewalks littered with fallen yard trees, scattered blue bird eggs, oranges blown off their stems, crackling coils of electric lines and the concrete itself broken into shards by the temblors? In my memory, the storms and earthquakes always happened at exactly the same time. All this threatening nature had a hapless boy in its center. The world seemed so bland now, not that close succession of natural events, ecological dramas that peppered my childhood seasons. Or perhaps, as I often suspected in the years that followed, I was the over-anxious child, unhappy in the real world, creating storms that were not there and dangers to color otherwise placid days.

Whatever went before, it felt right and good to be back beside the Pacific. I could feel creative energies inside me moving up like a geyser about to explode, and I knew I would be able to finish the second draft this summer. I walked back in front of the other cottages, still un-peopled, to Hayden's house. Beside it he grew a small kitchen garden I had not noticed before: lettuces, peas and herbs in front of the banana groves, behind a low chicken-wire fence to keep out the night creatures.

The mother of all century plants, five feet high and the same wide, grew right against the vegetable enclosure, against my side of the house. I looked down into the confluence of all the gray-green leaves and saw a purple-green nubbin pushing up from the center, an over-sized asparagus stalk. I wondered if it would bloom before I left at the end of summer, a candelabra of white blossoms to mark the finale of my editing.

At the writing table, I settled into the process that would occupy each morning. I faced away from the view of the ocean and looked through the pages at Laura's commentaries, written in the margins and onto the blank, facing page with a fine-pointed red pen, arrows reaching across to the pertinent paragraphs. Laura had been entirely right earlier in all of her comments on my collection of short stories, to expand a scene here, to close one down earlier there, to give more insight into what this character was thinking as his house caught fire, and to describe more fully this character's physical appearance. I knew to put aside the gripes that I harbored, not take the comments personally and make the changes she asked for.

You have created
some very intriguing characters
for the story, but I don't think
you have explored them
nearly enough.

This was a personal failing as well, because I knew that I ignored the characters of my own world, my friends and brothers who claim I never returned their calls, their urgent complaints forgotten. I did not love those around me enough, they told me.

Laura could see in my writing that I was this self-centered person, too inward-looking, much like the others who observed in the paint-strokes of my paintings that I was left-handed and slightly myopic. It was not comfortable to be looked at so closely, completely disrobed, rough elbows and skin eruptions obvious to all.

> *When you write about art*
> *or observe a location—*
> *the writing is wonderful. But you*
> *don't give your characters*
> *the same attention.*

Of course, I loved to talk about my art, myself, and what the landscape in front of me looks like. Now it should be an easy maneuver to turn it around to illuminate the rest of the book. Simple. It was just a matter of lighting, more wattage here and a pink bulb to soften the effect there. I had left too much in the dark, confusing those who asked for delineation and clarity.

At first the changes came slowly, grudgingly. I wrote my ideas in long-hand next to hers, in blue ink, such as "expand this section where grandmother is grieving." It was natural that I would have shortened the grief-stricken sections, as it was a subject I wanted to ignore in my own life. Why would I want to bring it up again and again?

> *Why did grandmother's*
> *lesbian episodes*
> *occur off-stage? Let us see*
> *what happens there.*

Was I ashamed of having a grandmother who loved another woman? No, of course not. And the years she lived with Simon, another painter, almost twice her age, why aren't they also included more fully? I grappled with these shortcomings in my mind, trying to find a way through them.

Simon appeared fully in my mind, but it was necessary to let the reader see him sitting like a kindly king in the middle of his world, his chair always in front of his easel. His presence in the studio every day was the pivot around which the family moved. The terrifying forces of war, death and deprivation, so omnipresent in my childhood, made sense if Simon just stayed there in our middle; if art still mattered in this mad world, then there was hope, maybe promise of change.

The longer I spent on these stage directions, the more I wrote along the margins, the more it became apparent that mere patching would not do. I thought of the impractical flat roof on my adobe house in Santa Fe, repaired annually by a handsome, mustachioed scoundrel as winter and rain weakened different areas each year, and the ultimate realization that I must give into his high-priced proposal to re-roof the house entirely. Patching would no longer do, either for my roof or the novel. I must start again and write the story anew.

Could I rewrite it totally in the three months that I was allotting myself? It did not matter because I *must* start again, using the first draft only as an outline and letting my expanded viewpoint dominate. It would be the opened peony, vibrant and fragrant, a full-blown deepest pink, instead of the tightly-wound, closed tulip, pure-white, odorless, of the first draft. Baroque instead of half-baked Zen.

The living-room door was to my back as I wrote and I did not hear Hayden open it. He said, "Dinner's ready." I half-jumped out of my chair.

"I didn't know you were cooking."

"I'm a good cook. Don't worry, you're in safe hands."

The table in the adjoining room was already set, two places with mats, plates, napkins, wineglasses, silverware, one place at the end of the table and the other nearby on the side. There were several platters of food, an opened bottle of white wine dripping moisture in the middle of the table, ready for our meal. It had all been summoned together from a netherworld, the kitchen, like magic, for all I knew.

I said, "Hayden, I'm impressed. Where did you learn to cook?"

"I picked it up. Mostly when I was a boy. Nobody else in my family could do anything in the kitchen, so it was up to me."

"Thanks. I didn't expect the room rent included a dinner."

"It doesn't, at least not every night. When I feel like it, I cook."

"Thanks, I understand. It looks great."

We ate mostly in silence, the sound of the surf a steady accompaniment to a red snapper fillet sautéed with almonds, rice with green peas, asparagus and a salad of butter lettuces from the kitchen garden. What a curious mix of traits Hayden was turning out to have—former surfer, talented carpenter, home-owner, an accomplished cook, a stunning beauty and loner who couldn't keep a girl friend.

7

Paillards in Basil Cream

It was a week later and the pattern of my days as a member of Hayden's household became more settled. He left for work at the power plant by seven each week-day morning, as I started my day with a walk along the beach. The rewriting of the novel was in the Churchillian stage of the End-of-the-Beginning, not yet the Beginning-of-the-End, fifty finished pages stacked up like trophy at the end of the table. If the stack grew each day, I knew my goal could be reached.

I tried to work for four hours in the morning and sometimes drove into town for lunch, other days making a sandwich and iced tea at the cottage. On good days I could work another two hours in the afternoon. I printed out, in forty-eight point type, a sign that I posted on the wall across from my writing table, lest I or anyone else who looked in forgot:

Mattox Williams is writing
a novel about a Santa Fe painter who faces
personal and artistic hurdles, love and loss,
while he contemplates what problems still remain
from his California boyhood.

Opening the well-thumbed and often refolded letter from Laura, I addressed another of her comments:

*He never confronts/deals
with the death of his family.
There are moments—glimmers—*

where he seems to, but he doesn't.
An event like this must have
a huge effect on a young boy.

This, I thought, was the major problem with the novel, a lack stemming from my own reaction to the major death in my life. It was the bulge in the length of a python, a meal eaten but not digested. My new version was now dealing directly with it, making the horrible power of death one of the themes of the first fifty pages, with occasional distractions into other matters. I must be careful, though, that death does not get diluted in these more diverting passages.

It was easier to solve the issue in a book, to put words to hidden thoughts, than to actually deal with it myself. I was able to write about death, add some fripperies, make the manuscript work, but the full knowledge of Richard's drowning was still firmly plastered away, unconfronted.

There were several ways that I repaid Hayden for his dinners. I bought the wine for every meal at the cottage and took the two of us out for dinners at the cafes in town, at least twice a week, sometimes as far away as Morro Bay. It appeared that we had reached an easy accord when I asked him about it while he was cooking one night. He had changed into his usual shorts and tee-shirt, wrapped the strings of a white chef's apron around several times and tied them up in front, a kitchen towel over his shoulder. He only lacked a chef's hat.

I sat down on one of the stools at the counter. I said, "I want to make things equal in our dinners together. Let me know if it's getting out of balance. I really appreciate them and want you to know that."

Hayden said, chopping onions with a long-pointed knife, "Mattox, I'm happy. Don't worry. I really like having somebody in the house when I come home. Somebody stable, that is. My last two girl friends freaked out here alone during the day."

"For me it's quiet and perfect for writing."

"Bridget, the last one, didn't think it was quiet here. She smoked a lot of dope, drank wine all day and got squirrelly at the wind whipping around the corners. The rustle of the banana trees made her feel creepy; it was like zombie music. There was a goodbye note left on the counter two years ago after she drove up to San Francisco. Too bad; she had great boobs."

With more brio than was needed, he swept the onions off the chopping board into a pan of steaming butter. Chicken strips went in on top of the onions.

"That smells good; what are we having?"

"Paillards in Basil Cream Sauce, fancy for chicken tits with white gravy."

"Do you miss Bridget?"

"For a while, I did. I miss getting laid on a regular basis, but I've got used to being here by myself."

"I live alone in Santa Fe. It's hard sometimes, in the night when you want someone to talk to."

"I wake up in the night all the time now. I think I hear something, somebody on the beach, a stranded whale, washed-up pieces of a wreck and what sounds like voices calling. One night I thought it was a fiesta, music and laughing, a crowd just outside my house. When I walk outside, look out onto the sand, there's always nothing. Then I go back to sleep."

"I believe that all thinking people wake in the night with worries."

As Hayden prepared the meal, I set the table with plates, wine-glasses, silverware and opened the bottle of wine. I looked over at him at the stove, expertly turning the paillards with a flip of the pan while he stirred a boiling pot with the other. I wondered if professional cooking, a chef's position, waited for him in the future.

There was an immaturity in Hayden, something unformed, awaiting a long-postponed spurt of growth. Our meals were not so silent as at the beginning. Hayden wanted to hear about how the novel was progressing, so

44

sometimes I described a section I had finished. I picked a passage I thought might resonate, be part of his experience. When the narrator, Donovan, comes back to his empty home, after his first days at a new school, unhappy and awkward, he listened intently.

On his own, Hayden brought up his life on the beach, often describing it with the lyric quality of a poet. He liked the winters here, even though California's were mild by most standards; he curled up early in the house, sometimes with a driftwood fire popping in the hearth, like a bear in his cave. Storms raged in the surf, but the cottage had survived on its slight elevation for fifty years; he felt safe here, hibernating while the strongest waves washed jetsam right against the doors.

He said, "Winter here goes away gently. The banana trees sit still without growing until the end of February, waiting for some sign. Then, on a single day, I'll see the new shoots start up all around the bottoms, hopeful and green. The Jamaican Reds are always first, dark maroon foliage popping up, then the Rajapuris and the purple Mysores. By the end of March all the trees are racing ahead; you can see them grow inches higher each day, big new leaves in a couple of days. I always feel excited at that time."

"When do you harvest?"

"Usually there are a few bunches ripe enough on the first of May. The Village Market buys all that I bring by; I just take credit instead of cash. Every few days I cut some more. By this time of year I have a large credit there. Our dinners come from the banana credit."

I lifted my glass. "I should give them a toast."

"We never have frost here, even though a half a mile inland it can drop to below thirty-two. It's a weather that belongs much farther south, like somewhere on the Mexican coast. I've often wondered if that means that I belong farther south, too. Where it's warmer, wetter."

"They say the best wines are in the far north of their growing regions. Like Burgundy and the Alsace. I think you've found your climate here."

"You think?"

"Yes. Most men your age haven't settled into a house and life the way you have. I admire that, your establishing a center."

Did I sound like Dr. Pangloss? The best in this best of all possible worlds. I had only wanted to put into words my approval of Hayden and his small sanctuary, to encourage him. I had learned, most of it during my time with Richard, to not leave praise unspoken. Anything can happen to prevent you from doing it in the future.

At other dinners I just read from sections of the book, and one night he asked me for more about the young boy, Donovan. I chose the passage about Donovan's first notion that his maternal grandparents, the McBanes, would not make room for him in their large, new house.

They tell Anna, his other grandmother, that he cannot stay any longer in their spare room since other family members from Minnesota will need it on their winter holidays. The vacations of distant McBane cousins were more important than a nest for an orphaned grandson. It is Donovan's first full awareness that he is really alone, a month after his own family drowned in a boating accident. This was not actually part of my life, but a bit of melodrama I added to color Donovan's later years.

Hayden said, "I can feel for Donovan. After my father died in Vietnam in 1973, my mother did not want to even look at us anymore, me and Sylvan. We looked too much like Dad, she told us. She married again, and after a couple of years said that she did not want us in her new home. She had a right to move on. It really hurt."

"Where did you live after that?"

"Ambrose, our uncle, took us in. I was about seven, Sylvan a year younger. Ambrose was a bachelor, but he made a place for us even though his small house was crowded. Our mother signed over all of dad's pension money to Ambrose, for our keep, so there was enough to pay the bills. She didn't care for the money, only wanted to be rid of us."

"That was difficult for a seven-year-old. Do you have a photo of your father?"

"Just look at Ambrose when you meet him. He and Dad were twins. Ambrose and Anderson."

"Identical?"

He nodded. "I remember Dad's face being stronger than Ambrose's, but on the surface of it they looked exactly the same. Maybe Dad laughed more. Ambrose can be very serious sometimes. Sylvan thinks they were like the dark and light sides of a coin."

"You said he teaches English at the college?"

"Yeah. Sylvan asked me to cook next week for all of us, so you'll meet him then."

We finished the rest of the meal and when we were collecting the dishes, stacking them to wash, Hayden said. "I noticed that framed photograph in your room. Is he your lover?"

"Was. He died last year. Drowned in Barbados."

"I'm sorry. He was very handsome."

"Yes." I got busy with the scrub brush on the plates and when we finished righting the kitchen, I said, "Thanks for asking."

8

Great Purple Stalk

What I had hoped would happen at Glitter Bay was happening. The morning mists worked their powers, nurturing the small memories that cannot survive in the thin, dry air of Santa Fe. I remembered the walks along the Laguna beach of my summers there, a ten-year-old up early to explore, dawn illuminating the sand-bottomed pools. Refreshed with each wave, the pools were clear enough to see the colonies of sea-anemones, waving acceptance of the currents. The boy observed that it may be a good life to be pliant like the sea-anemone, wafting this way, then that in the tide, waiting for patient hours until the fingerling comes too close, the first meal in a week. Do not fight the current, Mattox, give in to it.

The same boy first smelled the translucent strands of kelp there, washed up in ridges on the Laguna beach, and here again, there was that acrid odor. The same water birds, now thirty or more generations later, ran up the slopes at Glitter Bay with each rush of water, following them back down with sharp eyes for evidence from the air bubbles of a buried, bivalve breakfast.

If the mists made fertile ground for memories, I was happy to grow and bloom again after so long dormant. I knew my mind was expanding, opening closed chambers like a library opening the side rooms with the coveted, rare books, divulging knowledge so long hidden.

Returning from a walk along the beach, I found the neighbors that I had seen one day at the adjoining cottage, an old man and a girl, peering down into the century plant near my door. They were so absorbed in whatever there was in the center of the gray-green leaves that they did not hear me approach. The old man measured carefully with a yellow tape, a retractable carpenter's version.

I said, "Good morning. What's going on down there?"

The man turned around and put out his hand. "I'm Henry Clarence and this is my grand-daughter, Morris. We live in the cottage next door. I live here all the time but Morris is visiting me for the summer."

"You're lucky to have such a handsome grand-daughter."

"I think so. We're studying your century plant because it's going to bloom this year. A school report for Morris's home room."

He was older than he appeared from a distance, probably around seventy, very tanned, very wrinkled. His full head of white hair was cropped short, giving him a stern presence. The tanned face made his light blue eyes even paler, sharp like a hawk's. He must have been a very handsome man in his youth, a stunner my friends would have called him.

I said, "Is that what that purple nubbin is all about?"

"Yes. It will get taller and taller and taller, growing a few inches each day, slowly, slowly. Then, it will show its white blossoms up high like another sun, side blooms like so many arms."

The three of us followed his eyes up to where the bloom would be, a biblical incandescence yet-to-come. That Henry was accustomed to telling stories to children it was clear, an ability that was totally compelling, and into which I fell like a grade-schooler. We stood looking up in silence for a few seconds.

"But in the end, the whole plant will die and blow away," he said.

Morris looked unhappy, "Does it have to die?" She was also tanned. Dark-haired, in short pigtails, and blue-eyed, like her grandfather. Could their good looks be traced back to Ireland, blue eyes and black hair? Her eyes were earnest, worried.

He said, "It does, Morris. That is the way of things."

I asked, "How tall will it get?"

"Perhaps sixteen feet, that's about five hundred centimeters. A great purple stalk with a hundred ivory-white blossoms. Bees will circle around by the hundreds."

"I'm here for the summer. I'll give you coffee or orange juice next time. Just knock on the doors."

I left them looking down again into the conjunction of the leaves and returned to my writing table, and the new problems with my book. I was including fresh incidents in this new version, and I greatly amplified scenes that occurred only in passing the first time around.

There was a passage in the first draft that I had put off-stage, action happening elsewhere. It was a fragment that could be included as an aside in dialogue. In this new rendtion, I reassessed its worth upwards, more vital to the stream of the story, an episode that needed to be explored in full. I hoped Laura was smiling.

I spent several hours, spilling into the early afternoon, to insert this new scene, then took another hour to repair the edges where we entered and where we departed. If only for a moment or two, I was pleased with what I had wrought, happy that this addition appeared seamless, without art as I reread it. The book was going well.

After a late lunch, I decided it was time to telephone Wilfred Cooper. I had not updated him on my whereabouts or, more important to him, my emotional state. I turned on the cell phone and, after several attempts, it picked up a signal. I dialed his number.

"Darling, where in the world have you been? Did you just throw your phone into the waves? We were all so worried."

"I've come to ground in Glitter Bay."

"I know. Since we hadn't heard from you, I called Bob Dermott and he said you had no doubt gone there. I laughed when I heard that name! Glitter Bay, indeed. Sounds like a burial ground for drag queens."

"I've rented a room with a good writing table, French doors opening right out onto the beach. A perfect place to work. It's a family town, hidden away with no up-to-date amenities."

"Bob told me there is a nuclear power station nearby. Hardly suitable for our elegant Mattox."

"It's fine and I'm getting work done. I can see the sea as we talk, clean waves crashing onto pure white sand, mind you. No pollution whatsoever."

"Who are you renting from?" Nature and a description of its bounty were never of interest very long to Wilfred when a real person could be described.

"A single man, straight, very handsome, and for your information, a very good Cordon Bleu cook. He grows bananas beside the house, sells them locally."

"That doesn't sound so very straight to me."

"He is, I assure you. Glitter Bay is a real community, with honest working people."

"How dreadful. Bob said that it was, but I had hopes otherwise. I saw a dark-haired bachelor with cruel hands, a forgotten house on a cliff by the sea, a yearning to be loved. Something with Joan Fontaine."

"Nothing like that, honey. But I'm driving down to Pasadena in a week or so, and later to Laguna. There might be action there."

"Well, there's nothing new here, only another gloomy dinner at Kate's, frozen green peas with an under-poached salmon, which she dropped on the floor and in secret put back on the platter. I was the token gay, the rest all those broken-down CEO's and their wives that Kate seeks out. A really boring summer without you. How is the book going?"

"Well. I'm using Laura's letter as a guide and I've made major changes. Good ones, I think. Has she done anything for you?"

"No, just more rejections. I think I may have to do a complete rewrite, too."

"It will sell as it is, I know. Your illustrations are paintings in themselves, the best you've ever done."

"We'll see. Now, keep your cell phone charged, because I worry."

"I promise."

"I get distraught when I can't talk to our Mattox."

I realized that I had not thought much about Santa Fe and my circle of friends there, now several mountain ranges away, perhaps much farther in the miles of the mind. As I thought about them once again, the practical thoughts of a home-owner surfaced. Lettuces should be replanted for late summer harvest, lilies dead-headed (not cut back), and the roses could take a last good feeding.

I wondered if Olivia Montelle, between her soirees with arpeggios on the piano monitored the watering system, making sure that everything even in the far corners was getting water. Opera people were not good at gardens, I knew. I had just replanted those young horse-chestnut saplings, raised from the nuts that I smuggled through customs from Istanbul. They needed extra moisture the first year, encouragement to flourish in this land of the infidel. Worry, worry and more worry.

How quick the quotidian tides took hold, once you let them in. I thought about calling Olivia, to see if Ben was faring well, to ask about the garden, how the house was suiting her. It was five o'clock there, only a few hours before a week-day performance, not a good time to reach an opera singer. She would be crabby and in a hurry to have her wig adjusted. I would call when Sunday rolled around and she was lounging about in that kaftan, letting the obviously thirsty delphiniums wither while she and her musical friends downed more Bloody Marys, laughed at jokes only opera insiders could appreciate.

9

Super Paradise Beach

This was my fourth Saturday at Glitter Bay. The evening meal had become a ceremony, alternating between Hayden's cooking and my choice of the cafes on the highway. He fell easily into the pattern, pleased to have another person in his life. I knew that the years after Bridget fled to San Francisco had been lonely for Hayden, although he would not admit it in so many words. In addition to the physical order so necessary in his life, doors that worked, sharp knives, a clean kitchen, Hayden also wanted structure in his home-life, a family, however strangely it was composed. I supposed that I was Bridget's replacement.

On Saturday morning, he started the prep-work for a beef stew, the main course for the dinner that night with Sylvan and their Uncle Ambrose. From my writing table, with the door open, I could smell the ubiquitous onions being sautéed and there was the sound of the meat cleaver chopping the beef into cubes. I wondered if all good meals started with finely chopped onions. I was sure that the celery here would not be cut on the diagonal.

Hayden was, on the surface of it all, happiest in the kitchen, where I often heard him whistling softly. Cooking was his way of repairing the abandonment of his youth, supplying this alternate home and hearth for his small family. If he did not get the love he needed from his father, at least he could offer to others.

I had observed that people who are happy, doing the tasks they enjoy, often whistle or sing in an unconscious, repetitive way. A Mexican handyman who worked for me in Santa Fe, Ramiro, was an innately talented mason, humming or whistling as he lay stone, installed a brick terrace or mixed the mortar, but he was silent when I asked him to work with wood, any type of carpentry a chore. I learned to hire others to hang a door or plane off the bottom of an obstinate window. Innate masons do not make good carpenters.

After an hour at the computer, I saw Morris and Henry just outside measuring the century plant. The paragraph that I kept reworking was not bending to my will, so I stepped out to join them.

"It there botanical news?" I asked them.

Morris said, excitedly, "Eighty centimeters high." She pointed to the number on the tape.

Henry said, "I think this is going to be a record for the beach. Last summer Hayden had a tall one on the other side of the house, but this will grow taller."

I said, "He's busy in the kitchen, otherwise I know that he would say hello."

"I can smell something cooking. It's good to have you here and Hayden happy again."

"He wasn't before?"

"No. His girlfriends made him happy for a short while, but that Bridget was a hellion. We were all glad to see her go."

"He does seem happy. I was noticing that this morning."

Henry said, "Hayden is at his best when he's looking after someone else, and he's pretty good at making people happy. Don't you think?"

"Well, I'm gaining weight on his three course meals."

"I meant more than that." He winked at me. So there was a news network along the beach, a back and forth of ideas. The small town was weaving its web. It was amusing that the neighbors now pictured me as Bridget's replacement, making Hayden happy in some inchoate way and getting happiness, nurture in return. A straight engineer's assistant and an older, gay writer did not exactly fit the norm of a blissful seaside couple, but maybe California's parameters were wider, more inventive.

Morris picked up the clip-board with her century plant report, the tape measure, and she and Henry left. To get my mind focused on my own matters, I took another walk along the beach, then delved into the mainstream of the book again.

The young man, my narrator, was maturing, growing into the painter he would become. I enjoyed writing about art and artists, as Laura observed, and full paragraphs flowed out as easily as single sentences on other days. The boy was growing up and his talent spread outwards like the branches of a young tree. As the afternoon ended, I had seven pages, seventeen hundred new words, a record for my time at the beach cottage. I felt they were good, but the true judgment would await a rereading.

Hayden had already set the table for our dinner. I sat down on a stool at the kitchen counter, talking to him as he put the finishing touches on the meal. He asked about Henry and Morris, and I gave him an update on their project.

He said, "Henry is a good man. I took to him as soon as I moved here."

"He's very patient with Morris, showing her the nuances of nature."

"Some years there are dozens of century plants in bloom on the beach."

I said, "They chose the one outside your house to write about; it's ready to go right up into blossom, they say."

"You will see it flower before the end of summer." He finished scraping the last of the green peas from their pods and dropped them into a sauce-pan of boiling water.

Ambrose was the first to arrive, promptly at six. I figured that he was about my age, slimmer in frame, but not in as good condition. Most of the male English professors in my college years were a bit bent and awkward, like Uriah Heeps, and Ambrose was no different. He had an elegant, tatty air, like a suit from London worn past its time.

Hayden hugged his uncle warmly, put a hand on each side of his face, and kissed him quickly on the lips. I tried to remember if I had ever kissed any relative, distant or close, that way? Kissing and hugging were not practiced in the Williams family, a cheek-to-cheek hug with no touching of the body was fully sufficient to evidence love.

How tactile Hayden was, reaching out to touch, circling his hand around an arm to make a point. It was part of what I enjoyed about our dinners together, Hayden's closeness, his hand on my fore-arm. He postponed a comment until his hand made a firm connection, as if he feared that I would run off mid-sentence.

He introduced me to his uncle, describing me as the famous writer. He seemed proud to say that I was writing a novel in his house. Sylvan came in without knocking. She helped Hayden bring the food to the table, the stew in a covered tureen, a platter of rice and vegetables, another salad of perfect butter lettuces. We passed the plates around and served ourselves from the tureen. Ambrose was the first to speak.

"How is the book going? Is Hayden's house a good place to write?"

"Slowly but well on the first, excellent on the second."

Sylvan said, "Uncle Ambrose, would you know that Mattox is gay from just meeting him? I didn't." Was this Sylvan's punishment for me letting her down, not being the man she wanted?

He answered, "Gay people look just like other people, Sylvan."

"I think he's really good-looking, from the first time we talked in the bar, the sort I could really go for."

Ambrose said, "I wouldn't count on that if I were you, dear."

I wanted this line of conversation to stop. "You know that I'm not at all comfortable being talked about as if I wasn't here."

"Sorry, Mattox. You must be about my age. Did you serve in Vietnam or did you hole up in Canada with the other intellectuals?" Ambrose did not believe in gentle foreplay.

"I served in the Army, but not in Vietnam."

"A hospital nurse, then?"

"No. I was called up in the draft and went to basic training for the infantry in Camp Chaffee, Arkansas. I still have the marks from chigger bites. Because of a really wet winter there, I caught pneumonia. My lung collapsed. After three months in the army hospital, I was given a medical discharge. They did not want an invalid with one lung in their army."

"I didn't mean to make you into a draft dodger. Sorry."

"I have to say, I was not unhappy to be let out of the army. I had many issues with the war, but I would not have hidden away in Canada or burned my draft card. A lot of friends did, however. I admired their choice but could not do it myself."

"Hayden's father, Anderson, and I enlisted together, went to Vietnam as brothers. You could be assigned together if you enlisted. He walked out of base camp, twenty yards ahead of me and was blown into pieces our first week there. He was dead before he even had time to get his boots firmly on the ground. That's a great deal worse than chigger bites."

"I totally respect the men who went."

Sylvan interposed, "Ambrose asks everybody about Vietnam. Don't take it personally." I now saw the military vestiges in Ambrose's bearing, his hair too short for his age and his movements spare, thought out. A curious mix of Mr. Chips and a VFW regular.

Ambrose continued, "It was hard on all of us after Anderson was killed. I stayed on for the full four-year enlistment, but I knew that the Army was not the career I had hoped it was going to be. I entered university in Berkeley afterwards, a scholarship. I was the first in our family to go to college and I've been teaching ever since. English Literature 304 with Mr. Danning at the Morro Bay Junior College."

I said, "Hayden says you are a natural teacher."

"Sweet, dutiful boy. Tell me about your published book. Hayden said it is a story about artists."

"A book of short stories about Santa Fe painters. I wanted to write about what it is to stand at the easel, to make a living at art."

"I recall that I read a review of that somewhere. *New York Times* was it?"

"Good for you. It came in the New and Notable sidebar some

months after it was published, and it made a difference in sales."

"There was a curious, long title that caught my jaded, old eye?"

"*Why I Won't Be Going to Lunch Anymore.*" I was impressed that in faraway Glitter Bay, Ambrose read the book reviews in the Times; so many of my Santa Fe friends did not. For that matter, most of them read only a few of my stories in their inscribed gift copies, then put the book down.

"What does the title mean?"

"It's the title of the first short story about a painter who at lunch innocently sabotages an important painting sale by another artist, a friend. The nature of their friendship changes, and the painter knows that he won't be asked back."

"So you actually know painting and the painter's life?"

"I think so. I've painted in Santa Fe for twenty-five years, made a living at it."

"A writer and a painter. You're quite the man, even if the Army didn't suit. I honor both of those more than so-called manly pursuits."

"Me, too."

I could see that Sylvan and Hayden were very proud of their uncle. She said that teachers were well paid in California, at least those in junior college. Ambrose took every summer off and traveled to Europe, or to the Far East. He was leaving soon for the Greek Islands and he had spent most of last summer there.

I asked, "Which island?"

Ambrose said, "Mykonos. I stay at the *Poseidon Hotel* and rent a jeep, go swimming in the Aegean every day like Lord Byron. With the dim night light they provide at the hotel, I try to read the books for the fall term."

"I know Mykonos, too. My friend, Richard, and I used to go there. It has an easy ambience, good beaches, restaurants right on the water."

"Did you ever go out to Super Paradise Beach?"

"Every day. We went out there early before the crowd, swam all morning. Left as the people really started coming to the beach."

Ambrose said, "I was always part of the afternoon crowd."

Sylvan said, "Mykonos really agrees with Ambrose. He comes back with the best tan, looking happy and rested."

I realized that neither Sylvan or Hayden could have known that Super Paradise Beach was the most flagrant gay beach in all of the Aegean. Homosexuals from all over the world, although mainly from northern Europe, came there to meet and play, seldom clad in more than a signet ring or an armband tattoo. It was the meeting spot for the whole gay world.

Ambrose could talk about it to me, identify himself as a closet gay, and it would go right over their heads. He was just their adored, sexless, professorial uncle, the first of the family to make it out of the blue collar. But to me, he told of Lucullan nights, afternoons of cavorting, very little swimming. I doubted that many of his nights there were spent reading books back at the hotel, however dim the bedside light.

Ambrose's entry into the teaching world took him a step or two higher in class from his family, here in the supposedly classless America. I realized that part of Hayden's attention to me was a response to this obvious caste difference, the fascination of the working class for someone well-placed enough to take a summer off just to write a book.

I said to Ambrose, "I've tried other islands, Tinos, Hydra, and Patmos, but Mykonos is more comfortable, the place for me." If Ambrose was trying to communicate the secret signals of a hidden gay brotherhood, I would comply. It was difficult enough being an openly gay man, like me, but I knew it was immeasurably harder being a clandestine one, hiding from disapproval in an academic life.

He replied, "I go back whenever I can. It perfectly suits me, too."

Hayden, who did not comprehend, felt left out. He said, "Some year, I'd like to go with you. Maybe the three of us can go together."

"Maybe," Ambrose replied with a wink at me, "when you're older."

10

All Night Long

I spent every morning of the next week at the computer, the book growing at least a half a dozen pages each day, and Hayden, after his day of work, returned to the cottage for our evenings together. I had not expected to be so cosseted in my summer rental, revered like a Roman house god, a sacred presence in this simple abode.

It was late morning on Saturday when Hayden looked in on me at the writing table to ask about a swim. He said, "The best swimming is on the next beach, Pearly Gates we called it when we were growing up. We can stop in at Garnet's on the way. She has returned from San Diego where her daughter lives. You haven't met Garnet yet."

We walked along the sand with towels over our shoulders. It was a windless morning without fog, rare along Glitter Bay. Today the doors to Garnet's cottage were propped wide open, the closed curtains pulled back. She had returned to claim ownership of her beach, the real-estate duchess back in her castle.

We saw from the door that she was stirring a pot of soup on the stove. She heard Hayden's knock and, without turning around, said. "Come in, sweetheart. I'll make us some tea."

"Garnet, you old trout, I missed you. I've rented out the front bedroom while you were gone. This is Mattox, the famous writer, who is staying with me for the whole summer." Hayden sounded proud, as if he had caught a particularly fine grouper in the surf.

She kept stirring, turned only slightly towards us and said, "Welcome, Mattox, the famous writer." I could see she was not impressed with supposed fame. She was a small, very old woman who still stood bolt upright, no bending in her back. Like all the old-timers on Glitter Bay, her skin was tanned and wrinkled. What little was left of her hair was done up in tight curls, perhaps with the help of the more experienced beauty parlors of San Diego, and it was colored to the shade of a peachy straw. She wore slim-tailored pants and blouse of a matching bright pink, an orange kerchief around her neck. Wilfred would have called her a pulled-together old broad, a stringy mud-hen with style.

Hayden says, "What did you have to pay for that shitty hair-do? You always get into trouble in San Diego."

"Back off, Hayden, or I'll hit you with a pan. You know I can."

"I wanted Mattox to meet my favorite film star. Can you believe that when she was young she looked like a Spanish dancer, black eyes, long black hair and boobs to die for?"

I said, "She looks great to me." What else could I have said?

"Thanks, Mattox, but you don't need to get involved. Hayden and I enjoy our spats; they really are harmless. We know how to wound without bruising."

He said, "Garnet was big in the silent movies, but they fired her for her squeaky voice. They said the film world did not need another Minnie Mouse."

"He lies. I was always just a script girl, but I was good at it. The starlets came and went, while I had steady work behind the camera for almost fifty years. Never a year without a pay-check, even during the Depression."

I said, "Hayden said that you were with Cecil B. DeMille for a while."

"I did the scripting for all his early movies. After that, I moved on to other directors, other studios. I know a thing or two about money, so I saved what I could until I could afford to move here with my Frederick."

"Hayden also says you own all the cottages on the beach."

"Does he now? What a pretty-faced loud-mouth he is, telling all my secrets."

We took the pot of tea and cups outside, and sat down in the wooden chairs on the terrace, the windless morning with mist-curtained sun too delicious to ignore.

Garnet asked, "So you're staying for the summer, Mattox? You look sensible, and Hayden needs a friend living there to settle him down. Someone other than his dysfunctional family, that is."

She looked over to Hayden, pleased with her assessment of what he lacked. Despite the riot of color in her hair and clothes, she seemed to be a kindly, simple woman. She obviously adored Hayden, and he returned it.

I said, "I've rented my Santa Fe house to a soprano at the opera for the summer. Until September. I can't go back until then."

Garnet said, "Hayden needs a chum. Not old like me, but a man-friend more his own age." With sympathy she painted us with same brush.

"He's quite a bit younger than me."

"That's okay, because I can tell you're not old-spirited. You might as well be the same age."

Hayden said, "I've been cooking a lot, Garnet. We'll call you to join us one night."

"I won't hold my breath." She poured out the tea into our cups.

While Hayden went back into the house for the sugar, she switched to a confidential tone. "How's he doing? Really? I worry, you know, since his last girlfriend left."

"He seems fine, a true home-body. An uncommon trait in a man his age. I admire him for that."

"That crazy sister of his, she messes in his life too much. I've tried to bring him up to speed on her."

"How did he react to that?"

"He denied any problem there, of course. Said she loved him like a sister only. Nothing else."

"You think otherwise?"

"Indeed, I do. She's got the very illegal hots for Hayden, her own brother. They can put you in jail for that."

Hayden returned with the sugar bowl and while he stood, spooning out a serving for each of us, he said, "If Garnet had been born fifty years later, we could have generated real steam together. I would have made love to her all night long, so hard that there would be a script girl missing at work the next day."

She said, "He's a tease, Mattox, but who wouldn't have liked that? Except for the chafing. Loved all night long? Even you, maybe?"

"Even me, Garnet," I said. California people, including the ones in their nineties, talked about matters that were only passing mental fancies back in Santa Fe.

She continued, "Mattox, my dear Frederick is long dead. He could barely get up the muster to do it once a month, except when we were young. Bless his soul. But he adored me absolutely, never mocked me like Hayden here."

He said, "You love it. Admit it, you do."

"Okay, I do."

Hayden stood up and kissed her. She squeezed my hand with an extra strong touch, I thought. We said goodbyes and walked along the beach, heading down to the promontory and around to the next cove.

I said, "I see why you like her."

"She made it possible for me to own a house."

"She clearly loves you. A lot."

"Like your grandmother, Anna."

"No, not exactly like my grandmother."

"Yeah, she's different from most old ladies."

"She doesn't think too much of Sylvan, though."

"She says that Sylvan and I had a lot of sex together."

"You didn't?"

"We're brother and sister, Mattox."

"There would be nothing wrong with that. It seems natural to me for brother and sister to experiment, to try out love. A sibling is close at hand when the urge strikes."

"Maybe."

We reached the sandy middle of the beach. It was a small cove by Pacific standards, perfectly curved into a half circle of sand with a low cliff at its back. Grasses and wildflowers coursed down the ledges.

"Why is it called Pearly Gates?" I asked.

"Because so many people have drowned here. There can be a strong rip-tide, and when it comes with an undercurrent it can take people away. If you panic and fight it, you're lost. None lost this year, however."

"So why are we swimming here?"

"There isn't a rip-tide today. Only when you have the offshore wind. It's completely still this morning."

There were no other people on the beach, so Hayden took off his bathing trunks and rolled them into the towel, which he threw up onto the beach past high-water. I saw that he was the same tan all over as he ran through the shallow waves into the deeper water beyond. I repeated the process and followed him into the sea. It was much colder than I remembered from my boyhood; perhaps the waters of Laguna and Balboa Bay were enough farther south to have a warmth not here, or was my memory from childhood summers faulty?

We swam together out beyond the line of the surf, diving under the waves until we reached the stillness beyond. It was not as cold then, and I followed Hayden's swim path along the beach for several hundred feet. He was a strong swimmer, keeping a good Australian crawl form as he pulled ahead of me. It felt wonderful to be in the Pacific again.

We returned to the spot where we had entered through the deep water waves, and swam back to shore. The waves broke over us as we tried to race through the shallows to the sand, encircling us in a surge of cold foam. I spread out my beach towel and laid down in the sun while Hayden dried off, then he put his towel down next to mine.

He quickly went into a deep sleep. For half an hour we lay with the sun warming us up and I fell into the barely-aware state before sleep, the sound of the surf a soporific rhythm. I thought of seaside afternoons with

Richard in beaches around the world, in Mykonos, on the Kona coast, and the searing heat and green, piquant waters of Phuket.

Hayden woke enough to place an arm over my back, which brought me up from my daydream of Richard on other beaches. I felt that personal electricity that I sensed the first time we met. Was Hayden's arm on me an unconscious gesture of ownership or another of his tactile maneuvers, to prevent his companion from ignoring him? I thought about his taunting bit with Garnet, making love all night long. Imagine.

11

No Longer Skinny

I left the next morning for a few nights in Pasadena after I made order in my room, hung the dropped towels on bars and arranged the books in a line on my table. Hayden never locked the cottage, but I worried to leave it unlocked, he already at work up the coast. I used the key to lock the dead-bolts and replaced it above the door-light. The traffic intensified the closer I came to LA, long rows of slow-moving cars delayed the exit onto Sunset Boulevard, followed by an hour through late morning traffic from downtown to the easy bustle of Colorado Street in Pasadena. I felt a growing sense of pride that I had not lost the native Californian's ability to master the freeways. My learning to drive had paralleled the growing complexity of the roadways, the ability to course down the middle of seven lanes expanded as the lanes themselves multiplied.

I checked into the Oak Knoll Hotel, a rambling four-story establishment with red-tiled roofs dating from the Twenties, now going through its fifth or sixth rebirth as a five star resort. The swimming pool was green-tiled and cool, and the hotel was located in the middle of the three dozen streets I knew so well growing up there. I drove around the area for several hours, observing how little the actual streets had changed. As it got dark, I went back to have my dinner in the hotel dining room and got into bed early.

The next morning I toured more slowly around the streets of Pasadena, concentrating on those down the Oak Knoll hill. I used disposable cameras to record scenes and wrote down descriptions in a notebook of blue-lined paper.

The Pasadena of my youth was a town of a different spirit, when it and the nation were going deeper into decline, the Thirties making a deeper mark each year. Monies for paint, upkeep or anything new, were locked away in shuttered, Eastern banks; the Depression was slowly sucking the town's life away. It was a fond set of memories for me, however, the decrepit summer houses and overgrown gardens a paradise for an adventure-prone young boy and his pals.

I drove by the old Fair Oaks Hotel, which burned to the ground on Black Tuesday in 1929; the gardens, once expertly pruned and mown by squadrons of gardeners, were years later for me a personal playground of forgotten abundance. Camellias of all colors, planted as small bushes at the turn of the century, had by the late 1930s grown into trees. The grounds were impossibly overgrown, nurtured by the natural abundance of California. Groves of eucalyptus trees self-seeded into the former lawns and tropical vines had trunks a boy could climb.

As I slowed the car down in front of a house set far back from the street, an exact copy of the *Petit Trianon*, I heard my own voice as we fled in mock terror across the waist-high lawn grass, a creaky caretaker in pursuit.

> *"Run Jimmy, run. I think*
> *the old man next door heard us.*
> *He may have a gun."*

Young boys in crouched patrols looked back over their shoulders as they explored the hallways and sitting rooms, silent kitchens with north-facing windows, cook and scullery-maids long ago dismissed, eight-burner O'Keeffe-and-Merritts in pale green and ivory covered with bird droppings, and ballrooms with gilt side-chairs nestled into tall stacks, like so much kindling. It was a life preserved in amber, frozen still in the ochre light.

But no longer. The Pasadena of today had been discovered by young families, L.A. executives and design-savvy gay couples, the high windows re-puttied, elaborate wood trim painted with muted colors and driveways repaved with patterns of Mexican brick. Greene and Greene houses were now prized, spoken of with hushed reverence, their dark interiors as revered as ancient temples.

The wisterias that had almost consumed the pergolas in my youth were now tamed, pruned using the Penelope Hobhouse book as a guide, and the damaged crossbars replaced. Everywhere was the sense of a community rediscovered, the old genteel ambiance revived if not fully restored. I preferred the Pasadena of my youth, in disrepair, to this up-scale renovation. If Pompeii was uncovered by earnest museum workers, Pasadena came back from its decline with the aid of the young professionals, hoping their real estate investment would double in five years. It probably had.

I filled page after page with notes of what I saw, images and voices that I had forgotten in years focused on other locales, different parts of the world. I looked through the new to remember the old. Large houses which now looked small, great trees gone, not even stumps to show for them. I could hear my brother's voice:

"I climbed all the way to
Turkey Branch
and I could see the mountains."

Formerly empty side lots devoted entirely to lawn were now in-filled with new buildings designed to look old. The smell of orange blossoms settled like a ground-mist, drifts of erect calla lilies in the low, wet places, and the same shiny-leaved magnolia trees, now forty feet higher and as much broader, lined the driveways. Was that the tree where a cousin asked me to join him in a secret togetherness underneath its low branches, the first awakening of sex? He was two years older and knew the ways of the world.

"Let me lie with you in the shade, Mattox.
You'll like it.
Nobody will know. It won't hurt."

My elementary school had the same oaken doors, filling a gothic arch; they opened with a squeaky push of the brass bar and the redolence from the hallways inside brought the fourth grade back in its entirety, little girl-friends with tortoise shell glasses and mousey brown hair, whole conjugations of irregular Latin verbs perfectly recalled, the face of a geometry teacher with the most beautiful buck teeth, ivory and long, the incisors worn too smooth to be dangerous. I could see me in the classroom not wanting to put my hand up, not to be the smart-ass nerd with the first correct answer, but her sharp eyes saw that I had already finished. She knew that I knew the answer. I was her favorite, I was sure.

"Our Mattox has solved
the Seventh Theorem in four minutes,
so, class, put down your pencils."

When I returned to the Oak Knoll Hotel in the early evening, my mind was exhausted. Every turn had revealed voices and vignettes, pulling me back to when I was tender and unformed. I had forgotten that I was so unhappy as the boyhood experiences came back into focus. Another meal in the hotel dining room, a favorite of pearled matrons but few else, and early to bed, information-logged.

The next morning was bright and without smog. A swim in the hotel's pool would restore me, so I established myself at poolside with the help of the attendants, who brought me a stack of towels, glasses of iced-water and a cordless phone. National long distance only, they told me.

I had not called Laura with the regular reports that I had promised. Was it now a month since we talked, me acknowledging without comment on her answer machine the receipt of that annotated first draft? It was time

69

to face the music again, and since she was often at her desk in the New York morning, I called.

"Hello, Laura. It's Mattox in California."

"At last. I thought seriously about calling Missing Persons."

"I'm down in Pasadena for a few days, doing the research, but I'm staying for the summer up at Glitter Bay."

"The coast near Santa Maria? Why?"

"I rented a room from a local man. In a seaside cottage; it has doors opening right onto the beach."

"Sounds a delight. I have some interesting news for you, Mattox."

"Good news?"

"Good news. We have an offer from a classmate of yours, David Roth. He's the director at KableOne channel and they want to option your book."

"David Roth. I do remember him ⁄ a skinny, curly⁄haired boy with thick glasses in grade school."

"Well, he's still curly⁄haired with thick glasses but no longer skinny. He came by our offices himself with your book in hand. He thinks KableOne can do a handsome mini⁄series, one program from each story."

"That is exciting. Did you sign a contract with him?"

"You know I cannot do that without your signature. I believe that the money he offered is good, although not as generous as for a known writer. Roth was delighted that you were the same Mattox he knew as a boy. He said he was assured that they would exercise the option."

"Dare I ask, how much?"

"Thirty thousand dollars to start, for all two dozen stories. This is while they make up their mind. Then, when they decide yes, we'll write the actual contract. Residuals for re⁄broadcasts, improved monies if it catches on or they resell to other channels. We discussed an escalation clause. If they produce more segments, you will be asked first to provide more stories."

Was Dickens laughing? An early investment of a few pennies of kindness returned years later, innocent good nature rewarded with compound interest. David Roth from the fifth grade, the awkward boy for whom the basketball was an enemy had bloomed into the CEO of KableOne. At eleven years old I had grown to almost my full height, hormones atingle, while David stayed behind in the vulnerable state of pre-puberty, nerdy and be-spectacled.

Did he buy my stories as a silent repayment for my rescuing him from total defeat those many times? Which enemy was it, the tough red-headed bully who pounded his shoe on David's fallen glasses, leaving nothing larger than pea gravel, or the gang of Hispanic girls who chased him with willow branches, whipping his ankles with glee?

After my first time in the role of saviour to the weak, I had no choice but to continue. I pictured myself as a Saint Mattox, patron of the defenseless and be-pimpled. A long line of the helpless would follow me to waterside ceremonies to return their self-worth.

I said, "Can you fax me the contract here at the Oak Knoll? I have a machine in my room."

"Yes. Everything is a rush with the cable TV people. You should sign it and fax it back, but mail me the original. Roth did say that this will be a poor-boy project, no stars, no fancy sets. They will probably use locations in Santa Fe, studios and houses of actual artists there, because New Mexico gives them a tax break. A rental of your studio could bring you more income. They have their own, in-house script writers, so no film writing on your part required."

"That's a blessing. Tell me about KableOne. I never watch it."

"It's wholly owned by CBS, part of a package of channels they bought a few years ago. It came together with SportsNight, WOM, and MansBestFriend. CBS is hoping to upgrade their shows, using young talent, he said, more imagination than big budgets. They are buying books from debut writers like you, developing the scripts, and they will rebroadcast the shows heavily on all their channels, mixing back and forth. I read about this on their website and sent them a copy of your book. *Voilá.*"

"My thanks are in order."

"Accepted. Do you want to go over to Beverly Hills to talk with David Roth directly? He remembers you fondly."

"I'll bet. No, I'll let *you* do the talking."

"So, if you give me your oral agreement over the phone, I will call him today. We can follow up with the paperwork."

"I agree."

"By the way, how's the work on your novel?"

"I'm addressing each of your comments on my first draft."

"I did not mean to be harsh, only realistic."

"It's going well. Your comments, as usual, have been a great guide."

"You don't have to be smarmy. Let me know when you want to talk in more detail about it."

"I will."

I gave her the number of the fax machine and hung up. The contracts came through almost immediately, which I signed and re-faxed back to Laura.

With that bit of news, I decided to leave Pasadena with what I already had, a couple of notebooks full, and get back to work in Glitter Bay. There was just time enough to make it to the cottage before nightfall, so I packed up and headed out.

The village market was about to close for the day as I walked in. The produce section had a large display of Hayden's bananas, yellow, purple and red. I bought two frozen dinners, wine, coffee and something for breakfast, as Hayden was not expecting me back until the end of the week. The cottage doors were locked, so I put down the sacks of groceries and found the key over the door light. We had never locked the doors before; it was strange coming back to the beach house without its doors unlocked.

I unpacked the luggage while the frozen dinner was cooking in the toaster oven. Lean Salisbury Steak with Mashed Potatoes. Do Not Cook in a Toaster Oven. I was sure that Hayden would not want a packaged dinner, but at least it was there if he had not eaten. I wondered if he was at the Kamikaze Bar with the other workers.

In about an hour I washed up from the meal, dried and put away all the dishes. A repeat episode was all I could find on the television, a summer schedule of shows done over and over. As the credits were rolling at the end, Hayden came in the front door.

"You're back early. Didn't Pasadena agree with you?" He was clearly in a mood.

"I thought it would take four or five days, but it only took two."

"How was it?"

"It's all fancy now, new shops downtown, houses all tarted up."

"That's all of California."

"It's just new to me."

"Did you eat?"

"*Lean Cuisine.* Not your cooking, to be sure. There's another one in the freezer, if you haven't eaten."

"Thanks. I ate with Sylvan."

"I missed you, Hayden. It's good to be back here."

"Yeah."

I told Hayden I would turn in early, that I had some reading to do. I said good night and went to my room, shut the door. The new Proust translation that I had been reading proved denser than my tired mind could absorb, so I turned out the light. The idea that Swann's way was not my way, and Hayden's way was not mine either came to me as drowsiness started to win.

I went into sleep right away and proceeded to that deeply drugged state that comes right at the beginning of a night, as far away from awake as you ever were. With me, bombs might explode nearby without my hearing them. I woke up to a shaking of my shoulders, again and again. It was Hayden, sitting upright astride me, shaking, shaking. I could smell the beer on his breath as he leaned over me.

"What, Hayden, what?"

73

"Wake up, Mattox. I have something to tell you."

I could barely understand what was happening, the operative part of my mind in another world. "Hayden, get off me. Then we'll talk."

"I want to stay here until you listen."

"Okay. Okay. I'm listening." I rubbed my eyes with my hands, nothing in focus as it ought to be. He stopped shaking me and put his hands flat on my chest.

"Don't leave me again, hear? I hated it here without you." He leaned over me and I could smell his own aroma, animal and strong, under the beer.

"Hayden, get off me. I can't breathe." I had a sense of not wanting Hayden to move, even if I could not breathe, the hard planes of his body against mine. The sensuality of it brought me more quickly into awareness.

He said, "It was dark and quiet in the house."

"I was gone for only two nights."

"You can't go away again; at least, not right now."

"All right, but now get off me." He rolled over to my side, propped his head up on an arm. I knew that Hayden was playing with me, trying to control me. I was unhappy that I liked being played with, being the victim, the controlled one. I would have to think about that. I could all but smell the fear of small boy, a fear that I wanted to protect him from.

He said, "When I came home that first night and your car was not parked by the banana grove, my heart fell. It was the same when they told me Dad was not coming back."

"I'm sorry, Hayden."

"I thought that you had left me for good."

"I'm back now."

"I know that your world of books and painting will take you away again, but for this summer I want you for my own."

There was no response to that; how could I not be wanted? I wondered what serious fault lines had been cracked open in Hayden during my two-day hiatus, if after-shocks could be expected.

74

I said, "I have to admit that it feels good to be wanted, to be missed. I haven't had much of that in my life this last year. I won't leave you again." I knew it was a promise that would be hard to keep, but part of me wanted to try.

Hayden said, "I'll let you get some sleep."

"One more thing. I have to drive down to Laguna for the next section of the book. I don't want to upset you again. Why don't you come, too; we can make a week-end of it?" It would not do to have Hayden this out of sorts after every trip.

"When?"

"This Saturday, when you're off work. We'll come back late Sunday night."

"Okay. That sounds good. I've never been to Laguna."

12

Arugula and Butter Lettuce

As I sorted the papers out on my writing table to start the morning's work, I looked again at Laura's critical comments. There was a paragraph that jumped out at me, a new matter I would have to address:

> *There is much underlying sexuality*
> *that is intriguing, but waiting to be explored,*
> *either by the narrator or through the actions*
> *and conversations of the character. However, it seems*
> *dormant…there, but not there.*

I could hear Laura intoning those words, her well-modulated voice an enviable weapon in her daily dealings with the New York publishing houses. She had a way of getting right to the point.

Sexuality for me was there and not there. Just as grief was there and not there. Most of my emotional life was lived in the shade, under the ground, hidden rivers that did not stream upwards into artesian wells, but circled around restlessly under a placid sexual crust. Could dark and sensuous thoughts lurk under Mattox's sunny demeanor?

I had lived most of my life that way, admiring in others what the world pictured as the healthy Italian way, the blurting out without thought, quick to yell, quick to forgive. Too many of my ancestors from Northern Europe invested in me that mid-winter brooding, feelings kept securely wrapped in moist Stockholm newspapers. They stayed under cover, even in these days of sun and sand despite blond temptation in the adjoining bedroom.

If I could not change it, at least I learned to live with it, my subterranean sexuality. I had done that for years, but Hayden was causing something in me to change. He exuded a naked energy, a force field that trapped me every time he chose to turn it on. The magma in me was rising, the old dormant volcano about to surprise everybody.

Just as I turned on the cell-phone, to see if the battery's charge had held, it rang in my hand and I almost jumped out of my chair. I fumbled for the talk button and said, "Hello?"

"Mattox, it's Olivia Montelle."

"You're up early, Olivia."

"No performance last night. I wanted to up-date you on your house and your Ben. Don't be alarmed, he's okay."

"Does he come out from under the sofa now?"

"He's blossomed under my care, a new opera-loving cat. Whenever I can, I roast him a few North Sea shrimp wrapped in small bits of bacon."

"He will be a monster when I return."

"I was mad at him yesterday, however. He limped home late from a tom-cat fight somewhere across Canyon Road, even though I know you've had his war-mongers cut off."

"I guess they didn't get it all."

"I let him lick his wounds on a cushion while I practiced. He sings along for a while, then gives up in a snooze. He prefers Mozart to Verdi."

"He gets that from me. So everything is okay with the house?"

"It's paradise, as you know. My opera chums and I have dinner on the loggia, which I adore, by the way. Arugula and butter lettuce from your kitchen garden, scallions and the French beans. No tomatoes yet, but they promise to ripen soon."

"So you're liking it there? I'm glad."

"As I said, it's Eden. I've cut absolute armloads of flowers and the borders look as full as ever. I can't think why you gave it all up for the summer, but I'm delighted that you did."

"I do miss the place, but have comfort that it's being well looked-after. Let me take you to dinner when I get back."

77

"I accept. I feel I know you well. Your house whispers your secrets."

"Nothing like a bookcase to betray its owner."

"Best to you, dear, I must start my practice. Is your book taking shape? Are you dealing with the impossible loves?"

Olivia had a good memory. I said, "Yes to the first, I don't know to the second."

"May I read it before it goes to the publishers?"

"If it goes to the publishers."

"I have no doubts." She clicked off.

Why did I leave my little Heaven on Earth, with a resident Bengali, spotted not striped, the sanctuary of a walled garden, bursting now with summer succulence, in the very middle of Santa Fe's hurly burly? All this given up for a poorly furnished bedroom in a windy cottage by the sea, with a blond Heathcliff to contend with, waking me from sound sleep to reassure him that his father-surrogate will not leave again.

I could have rewritten the first draft as easily, surely more comfortably, back in my Santa Fe cloister with the doors thrown open to the garden, birds sometimes flying inside by mistake, circling from room to room. Nature pressed close in that garden, squirrels tip-toeing past the sleeping cat and the perfumed promenade of skunk families late at night.

The entire collection of short stories was written there, one summer through the following winter. Maybe I required a renunciation for my grief, a folk cure from time beyond time. Give something up, something you treasure. The death of a lover required the rending of clothes, the pulling out of hair and the breaking of plates on the ground. If you do not hurt yourself, you have not really grieved and thus cannot move on. I heard the wisdom from centuries of keening women in black bombazine, egging me on, urging me to slap the whips against on my back. Harder, my son, until it draws blood.

13

Armenian Eyes

The freeways on Saturday morning were less congested as we made record time down to Laguna with Hayden driving. If I imagined that I had regained my mastery of the California road system, watching him maneuver across the lanes, zooming into open stretches and matching the speed limit to avoid radar convinced me that I had a long way to go. Four hours without stopping and we pulled into Laguna's main street, Highway One, with the antique traffic signals in place in the center of the roadway.

Laguna was on the surface unchanged from my boyhood summers; the old hotel in town center, still a pile of unwelcoming gray concrete, was our starting point. I had phoned in a reservation mid-week, but it was too early to check in. Hayden found a parking place on the immediately adjacent street, a position next to a corner that I would have shunned.

Unlike my early years on the beach, there were now mahogany beach lounges with cotton cushions for rent by the hour, and a waiter from the hotel bar circulated among them for drink orders. It could have been the *Plage Privée* on the Promenade Anglais, where every chair was filled with white, long-faced people from Stockholm or round, pink ones from Hamburg.

We changed into our swimming trunks and raced to the water, a few degrees warmer, it seemed, than Pearly Gates. This time, I led the way for Hayden and we swam towards the promontory rocks where I learned to pull abalone off their submerged hiding places. I looked down in the clear pond, but I knew there were no abalone left in Laguna waters. Perhaps they hid on the difficult rocks along the western shores of Catalina Island, but too many eager fingers had put a finish to their time on the mainland.

After half an hour of floating, diving, sprinting, we swam slowly back to where we started and regained our rented places in the row of beach lounges.

I said, "What do you think, Hayden?"

"It's a lot fancier than Glitter Bay. I'm glad we came."

"Me, too. This afternoon, maybe we can just walk around town. How does that sound?"

"Great. If you don't mind, I'm going to join the guys over at the volley-ball game for a half-hour or so."

I stayed on in the deck-chair, absorbing the warmth of the noon sun. I resisted the soporific rhythm of the waves, stayed awake and people-watched as the beach filled up with day visitors.

On the promontory to the north of the beach, I could see the vine-covered studio of my grandmother's lover, an English painter named Latraviata Johns. Although impeccably English, she went to primary school in Berlin when her father was a diplomat of high rank there. She often reverted to the language of her childhood, eight years of instruction in High German. I remember her exclaiming "Ach" at the easel, when she painted a clumsy stroke. Beethoven and Bach played on the Victrola while she painted, and she openly mourned the loss of her Old Germany to the Brown Shirts.

"Mattox, come sit by me whilst I paint."

"What is that in the upper corner, an angel?" I asked.

"Or a demon. Just be silent and look. Some day you will need the secrets that you see."

I watched her for many hours, she oblivious to anybody else in the studio. Unlike the way I paint now, she started in the upper left corner and painted down to the lower right, finishing the canvas completely as she went. She rarely went back to correct a shape or darken a color. As I walked along the beach I heard her voice again, clipped and well-bred.

"Needless dithering is bad.
Say what you must, and move on."

"Are you humming over there, Mattox?
Please be quiet or
I'll send you back to Anna's cottage."

"You have the hands of an artist, son.
Don't disappoint them."

I struggled against her dogmas for many years as I tried to develop my own technique, sure that Latraviata's way was the only way. What an English aristocrat could do, a young art student could not. The message that she intended to pass on was that there was a way for me, also....not necessarily the same as hers. I can see her, erect, patrician, completely absorbed in the canvas on the easel. It was the world that I sought for myself, an island where wars, political intrigue, fashion and love swept around but not through. Santa Fe had offered that to me, a place where I could paint, be productive.

Latraviata's house was now barely visible behind shrubs and palm trees grown much taller and the frangipani trees that I knew laid down blossoms in a dense mat. The terrace was still there, where she, Anna and I watched the winter waves crashing on the rocks below, all of us in deep respect of the tempest.

I looked back at Hayden with the other volley-ball players as I set off down the beach. The beach lounges and sunbathers on towels thinned as the beach curved around under Latraviata's cliffs.

Although it was seldom unlocked in my time, maybe the stairway up the cliff to the studio was open. It was worth a trip down there to see, nonetheless. I walked along the edge of the surf, veering up as the waves came in and following them back down like the water-birds. The gate was locked, the old sign repainted with Latraviata's curious wording, *Always This Gate Is Locked*, as if it had been poorly translated from the German original.

When I started back up the beach to the hotel, a man walking the other way came over beside me, turned to walk in my direction and said hello. He had the vestiges of a swimmer's body, now a touch too ripe from the good things in life, but still lanky and trim. He was dark-haired and olive skinned, his pale brown eyes almost a deep yellow. Laguna had a big Armenian community when I was young, and he might be from a later generation: their dark looks, almost Turkish, a contrast to the typical tow-headed Californian. His tan, I was sure, covered every bit of his body, even the buttocks and the inside thigh.

"I saw you renting the beach-chairs with your friend."

"We're here for the week-end."

"Are you from LA?"

"No, Glitter Bay." It was probably easier not to explain the summer rental.

"You guys have a house there?"

"It's Hayden's, actually. Are you a townie?"

"I have the restaurant on the main street. Dominic's"

"And you are Dominic?"

"In person. If you want, I'll save you a table for tonight."

"That sounds great."

"Under what name?"

"Mattox."

"So you're the friend that Bob Dermott called about."

"You're Dom Histriodes. He said that he would call you."

"I'll look forward to tonight, Mattox. About eight."

I shook his hand, long-fingered, firm and slightly moist. We walked together back at the center of the cove, where he weaved his way quickly back through the lounges to the shady doors of the hotel. I lay down in the sun, this time giving into the delicious fingers of sleep as they crept downwards from my brain to all my body.

82

The volley ball group took a break and Hayden came back, breathing heavily. He sat on the foot of my lounge, shaking my leg to wake me.

"Childish, isn't it? I used to love volley-ball so much. Makes me remember the high school days." His eyes were dilated with the excitement of the game. He had tied a bandanna over his head, knotting it in the back with a quick expertise, giving him the youthful air of a high school team captain.

I said, "You played like you knew what you were doing."

"Glitter Bay was the state 4A champion, three years running."

"I can believe that. I walked down to the point, but the staircase was locked."

"Who were you talking to?" He turned to look directly at me.

"His name is Dominic. He owns the restaurant on the main street."

"It's so easy for you to talk to people."

"He was the one who first said hello."

"What did you talk about? I have a problem talking to new people."

"Nothing much, but he's saved us a table for tonight. You'll meet him then."

After lunch on the hotel's terrace, it was check-in time. We retrieved the stashed luggage and went up to our room, an ocean-front historic suite with a small balcony for watching the sunset. It was airless, stuffy in the room, so we opened the doors to the balcony. I suggested we explore the town, let the room cool.

We walked around the few streets of downtown Laguna, bulging with galleries, bars, restaurants, shops full of seasidery. The town was awash with summer visitors, sidewalks three abreast with tourists in shorts and beachwear, cell-phones ringing and youngsters listening with earphones to their own musical world. An hour of that and we both had had enough.

"Do you feel like a walk up-hill? Only a few blocks, but steeply up," I asked.

"Sure. Where?"

"It's called Waterbird Lane, straight up to my grandmother's old beach cottage. Five or six blocks."

We found the connecting road and then trudged over to Waterbird Lane. We were both sweating by then, I remembering the walk as easier, shorter and flatter in my youth. The cottages on both sides of the lane were bulging with the summer rental-people, windows open to family gatherings, towels drying on the picket fences, surf boards in a cluster against the shingled walls. Laguna had become one of California's ultimate beach rental communities, a week's rent more than twice what I paid Hayden for the whole summer.

At last we were there. Santacasita. It was grandmother's woodland cottage in the seaside setting, dark brown shingles with forest green trim, casement windows propped open on hooks for the breeze yet to materialize. All of her houses had that Black Forest quality, as if they had been kidnapped from the deep woods and held hostage in the ocean sun. They were shady and cool inside and was I wrong to remember banks of mosses and ferns on the northside?

The sign by the door was still there. SANTACASITA, in block letters.

"What does that mean?" asked Hayden.

"Sacred house, or maybe sainted cottage."

"Was your grandmother like a saint?"

"No, far from it….but she was, for a while, a minister's wife, and she built this beach house with the money he gave her from his marriage and baptism fees."

"He gave all those to her?"

"Grandfather said that they belong to her by ancient right; the Anglican pastor paid his wife all the sacramental money. In England, the wives bought land, cattle or silver for the house, but it was theirs to do as the please with. A bishop's wife could stash away a major fortune."

"And your Anna built her house by the sea. I would do that, too, if I was a minister's wife. She must have been a neat lady."

"I think she loved me very much. I certainly remember her that way." I thought of the family of carpenters and masons who built the house, a large clan of Mexicans who took pride in their work and were honored that they built it for the wife of a priest. It was almost as good as building it for the priest, himself, they told her. The curiosity of a priest with a wife was often the talk as they built.

"You're a lucky guy, Mattox. To have a family that loved you."

"I know, but I've observed that just having a family doesn't mean they love you."

"Tell me."

As we walked back down to the hotel, I remembered the many times that I walked over to Latraviata's studio from Santacasita, sometimes to pose for her Biblical paintings, a shepherd boy in a singlet and sandals and sometimes to just watch her paint. Anna came on some days, bringing a hamper full of lunch sandwiches and deviled eggs; I sat in the sun while she and Latraviata laughed at their whispered secrets. It was a golden time surrounded with loving elders. Or was this my mind-washing machine at work again?

14

A Rock from the Sky

The balconies on the beach front of the hotel were full of guests waiting for the sunset, an established ceremony now, with people watching from all of the beach chairs below. The sky was clear with no storm clouds on the horizon to obscure the sun's slow dip below the edge of the world. The last crescent of deep orange slithered down out of sight, no trumpets, no flourishes, only an *a capella* sigh from the audience, scattered applause. In tropical waters, people expected a green flash, but we were too far north for that.

I got up from my chair and said, "What do you say? A drink before dinner?"

"Fine."

Standard Laguna dress-code at night for men was a short-sleeved Hawaiian shirt, loose, a pair of shorts, flip-flops or loafers, no bare feet. We headed down the street to Dominic's, where the flashing green of a neon palm tree served as the apostrophe in the sign. It was a major establishment, with a well-chaired waiting room, a separate bar, and many dining rooms protected from trespassers by the head waiter's station, where a woman you would not like to argue with presided. All parts of Dominic's restaurant spoke of a well-run operation, profitable, a year round business, not a summers-only place with blank-eyed college students in charge.

I led the way over to the bar and we found two vacant stools in the middle of an otherwise packed bar; all of the small tables were encircled with patrons waiting to be called for their places in the dining rooms. Hayden ordered a beer and I asked for a scotch and soda with a twist. The woman next to him turned and starting talking. Apparently Dominic's was not just a gay bar and restaurant.

While the bartender mixed the drinks, I walked over to the woman who guarded the gates to the dining room, to insure that Dominic had remembered. I gave her my name and she turned like magic from the fearful-haired Brunnhilde to a welcoming matronly type, an impressive example of the power of insider trading.

"Dominic asked me to save the best table for you and your guest. The only two-top with a view. Are you ready to sit down?"

"We're having drinks in the bar. About ten minutes?"

"As long as you want. And, by the way," she paused to get my attention.

"Yes?"

"I haven't seen Dominic so excited in months." She winked.

Back at the bar, Hayden was completely beguiled by the young girl next to him; I saw her laugh and throw the hair away from her face, body language of a woman on the make. We spent ten minutes that way, me looking down into my drink and Hayden chatting up his neighbor. When I heard a lull in their conversation, Hayden turned to me, asked if our table was ready.

We were seated with a flourish. There was a full view from our table high across the highway to the water, the premier seats in the house. Dominic's was a steak and lobster sort of restaurant, with a long menu of side-dishes such as foil-wrapped baked potatoes, big as river rocks, signature salads with red lettuces and orange tomatoes, several vegetables of the day, each separately priced. Dominic knew how to make money in the food business.

Hayden suspected that he had ignored me too long at the bar, so he came up with some personal questions. "Tell me what your sale of the stories to KableOne means."

"I don't really know, Hayden. It is a nice pile of money that I did not expect, for no extra work."

"Does your agent get part of that?"

"Of course, but she earned it, even though the CEO at KableOne was in grade school with me. David Roth, one of those helpless kids when he was young."

"Do you think he bought the book because he knew you?"

"I think so."

I told Hayden about my exploits with David Roth in our school days. I continued to wonder myself if this was not just a payoff. Hayden said he could understand David's appreciation, why he would want to repay so many years later.

He said, "I didn't have an older brother, someone to protect me from danger. Dad was dead, and Ambrose wasn't there during the day, when you really needed a brother. That's what you gave to David, a safe place."

"I suppose that's exactly it. It was not right for the others to beat him up, though, to humiliate him. I could put myself in his place, and it was easy for me to break up fights. The other students, bullies included, backed off from me since I was so big for my age. A good thing, and a bad thing."

"Why bad?"

"I was a foot taller than everybody else, different, intimidating. Kids don't want to stand out."

"I wish you had been my brother."

"Me, too, Hayden."

He ordered a New York Sirloin and I asked for the abalone steak, in memory of the many meals out in Laguna restaurants with my grandmother. If she found the abalone to be tough and rubbery, as it usually was in those days, she sent it back to the kitchen, with instructions for its tenderizing. We often had to wait another half an hour before it came back. "Never mind, Mattox, they won't get it right if we don't complain. All of France does that and that's why they have such good food." Latraviata always ceded to grandmother in matters of food.

Thanks, grandmother. This time it was tender and seaworthy, maybe thanks to the passed-down fear of the imperious old lady who lived in the hills, a legend from kitchen to kitchen. Hayden continued, "Will you write the scripts yourself?"

"No, thank god. They have staff writers who will render them into one hour segments. Laura said there would be more royalties when the programs were re-broadcast, more if they are shown on another channel and I would be paid for any new stories they used."

We finished our meal with an order for double espressos. Dominic himself brought the cups to the table, the *eminence gris* who watched everything from the sidelines and stepped in for ceremonial effect at the meal's close.

He said, "Mattox, what do you think of the place?"

"A great dinner with a tremendous view; we couldn't ask for more. Dominic, this is my friend, Hayden."

Hayden stood to shake hands with Dominic. I looked for any expression of dislike on either face, but both were blank. If the night would include shows of envy or chemical aversion, at least it was starting on a flat field.

Dominic said, "Let me buy you guys after-dinner drinks in the bar."

We agreed with more hand-shakes, and, after refills on our espressos, left the dining room. The bar was now cleared out, most of the tables empty and the same woman still reigning at stage-center in the bar. Dominic sat on a stool at the far end, so I took the one next to him. Hayden rejoined the woman, who laughed a bit louder and shook her hair again.

Dominic said, "Thanks for coming by. I'm glad your friend is straight; it might make things easier for me." Dressed up for work, Dominic had a sense of authority, ownership that eluded him on the beach. He wore expensive black trousers and a black silk shirt, open two buttons down to show a tan chest and some gold chains. Black silk and gold suited his Mediterranean coloring. I had tried the same look but usually felt that people knew it was wrong, as if I had stolen the whole ensemble earlier that day from a fallen Greek, too weak to put up a fight.

I said, "I'm renting a room from Hayden for the summer. Glitter Bay is a perfect place for me to write; few distractions, foggy mornings."

"I'll bet. What are you writing?"

"A novel. Part of it is set in Laguna, so I came down to reconnoiter, to remember."

"You belong here, not there. Glitter Bay isn't for the likes of you." He spoke the name with a disapproving emphasis.

"I wouldn't get any writing finished here. There are definitely distractions here."

"Have you ever had a lover?"

"Yes. He died last year."

"I'm sorry, Bob didn't tell me. How long were you together?"

"Twelve years. He drowned in Barbados. A good swimmer, but washed ashore dead anyway. Natural causes, the coroner said." Why was I giving up tender information so quickly? Was Laura's comment about my submerged sexuality being addressed by an adult portion of my persona, the one that took her criticisms to heart?

Dominic said, "It's been a hard year for you, I know. My lover died four years ago."

"How are you dealing with it?"

"Not well. I thought the second year would be better, but it wasn't. So I just keep going, purposely working longer hours here."

"Because of your eyes, I wondered if you were Armenian. I remember several large, happy Armenian families when I was a boy here. You look like them, handsome and dark."

"I wish I was, since you seem to like them so. No, my father came from Cyprus to work in the vineyards around Napa. He and my mother eventually went back, but my brothers and I stayed on. We were born here in America."

"Do you ever go back there? To Cyprus?"

"So many questions. Let me ask you some. Are you in love with your friend Hayden over there? You seem to be. He has a wandering eye, can't be faithful. And he will use his attractiveness to women as a weapon.

90

Nothing will come of him but unhappiness, you know."

"I suppose."

"I know. Instead, you should let me be your lover. At least for tonight."

"We've just met. How do you know that I could be your lover?" I wondered if I had a flashing sign over my head, invisible to me, but openly advertising to all others that This Desperate Man Is Back On The Market. There was the body-builder who offered me Nirvana in Palm Springs and now Dominic, perhaps offering the Cypriotic version if I relented.

He said, "It doesn't take long. My mother said that all Cypriots believe in signs, an animal or person who bumps into your life with a message; she told us to pay attention to them."

"I almost believe in them, too. Richard did. How do you know if I qualify as a bona-fide omen? I could be an imposter, a false messenger, merely a confused bird who strayed off the straight and narrow."

Dominic smiled. He obviously enjoyed a bit of wordplay, dancing about before coming to the point. It was one of Richard's qualities, too, that I grew to savor, to never to say up front what he could say later with more effect, to fool around with words. In the banter back and forth, desire grew.

"Mama said that an omen hit you like a rock from the sky."

"I don't see any bruises."

"It just hit me a few hours ago. I'll be all black and blue tomorrow."

"I like you, Dominic. Can I come back here on my own, after the summer?"

"Of course, but it would be better if you just take my hand now and come away."

Hayden left the blonde woman and came to sit beside me. "What have the two of you been talking about?"

I said, "Love and lust."

"Me, too, with Cynthia down there. She wants me to go back to her place."

Dominic said, "Why am I not surprised?"

"I'll see you tomorrow, Hayden," I said. He hugged me across the shoulders with his arm and walked back down to Cynthia's stool. She waved pointedly to me as they walked out of the bar, as if she had won the first prize and I had lost. Perhaps she had.

Dominic had a big smile and raised eyebrows as I turned to him. "So this clears up the schedule for Mr. Mattox, I suppose?"

"I would rather wait until September, Dominic. Is that okay?"

"Poor me, now all black and blue for nothing. I'm sure you will be worth the wait."

"I don't know."

"I do. Will you come by here tomorrow before you leave for Glitter Bay?"

"For sure."

15

Glorious Summer

I walked around, not directly back to the hotel, but past the galleries and shops of Laguna's center, still lighted in expectation of night customers. The gallery rents in town center had sky-rocketed over the years, but the paintings, generally seascapes and waterside scenes, were not of the quality of the halcyon years. Laguna had become the lowest common denominator art town, everything immediately available to the dimmest mind.

It was sad, because I remembered the spirited conversations about art in my grandmother's house, a boy trying to keep up with the excitement of artists talking about their work, their dedication to what they did. Simon with stories about a painter's life in Berlin between the wars, his struggles with making abstraction his own, Latraviata with her mystical views of the painter's responsibility, and the other artists who spoke of the quest of excellence, the ethics of the easel. From what I saw in the lighted gallery windows, that spirit must no longer exist in the eucalyptus-shaded studios in the hills above the town. If art had died, commerce had not.

At the hotel I went to sleep almost immediately, a tiring but exciting day behind me. Sometime after midnight, I heard Hayden come in, noisily shed his clothes and get in the other side of the bed. He put a pillow over his head and I went back to sleep shortly after I heard him start his heavy breathing. For a moment, I wondered what had sent him away from Cynthia's nest, but sleep pulled me back before any resolution.

There was a dim light of morning from the window when Hayden slid over, threw an arm over me and nestled his face against my back. It was a galvanic wake-up for me, no alarm clock needed, as the full length of his body pressed against mine, his firm warmth against my entire length.

How many minutes did I lie there, not moving, bringing in shallow breaths to preserve the moment, not knowing what to do next, as the touch from his arm suffused me? He was not snoring, so I wondered if he was feigning sleep, his erotic thoughts floating like sea-birds above the water, just like mine. I heard the sounds of the surf crashing onto the sandy beach, an insistent, sensual cadence again and again, a rhythm that began in me as well.

I turned around to embrace Hayden completely, to face frontally whatever this meant. I shed my pajama-bottoms and slid a leg under his, pulling us closer together, the other leg going naturally between his. He had gone to sleep without clothes and he was now as hard as I was, and I could feel the throb beneath his skin as I pressed closer. Wait, Mattox, just wait and enjoy it, let the morning take its own pace, because it will probably stop when he wakes fully. This is only a mistaken scene from his fantasy world of waking up.

The tan solidity of his stomach pushed into mine as I stayed firm against him. Without seeming to wake, he started a movement back and forth, slowly at first, sliding over me with long strokes. I could picture myself a man astride a horse, the undulating caress gaining speed, becoming, ever so slowly, a persistent canter. I pressed into the ride, responding to his rhythm with an equal force. It was only a few minutes, but much longer in my body clock. If there were five weeks of desire for Hayden stored up inside me, hands that stroked my arms, smiles that looked right into my brain, a yearning looking for a way out, they now let themselves loose, a letting-go that rippled an electricity up my spine and over my head.

With eyes still shut, Hayden's pace picked up, now finding a smoother course for his regular thrusts, then slowing down to long, purposeful moves. I could feel the strength of his legs as he brushed mine. I matched his timing, going backwards, then forward when he retreated. Even if he

94

was, in fact, asleep, Hayden was a pro at love. A few more deliberate, long glides across me, like a violinist's bow across his strings, and he joined me in an excited finale.

I lay there for how many seconds, not moving any part of where I joined him, then gradually, gently, extracted myself. I got up from the bed and went into the bathroom, put a face cloth under cool running water, and returned with it and a dry towel. I washed Hayden off, and dried him with the bath towel. Was it a thousand times that I washed Richard the same way, silently drying him, our roles set? Hayden was awake now, watching me, and when I looked up at him, he started to laugh.

He said, "You would think I got enough last night, wouldn't you?" He did not look at all sleepy, eyes open with amusement.

"So you didn't?"

"We humped away for an hour or so. Cynthia made a lot of noise and clawed my back, the neighbors called to complain, but nothing happened."

"I guess I'm the lucky one."

"Mattox, you're more of a man than you look like when you're dressed. That was good. Thank you." I remembered when I used to thank Richard when we were exhausted from love. He said that true lovers should not have to thank each other, it was like thanking yourself.

"Thank you, too."

While I showered, Hayden went down to the beach for a swim. I dried myself standing on the balcony and watched him beyond the breakers, seeing my grandmother forty years ago watching me in the water from the same spot, finally calling out softly to come in now, Mattox.

She always ordered the sliced oranges and a bowl of Irish oatmeal for me while I showered off the salt-water; then I joined her at a white-clothed table in the dimly-lit dining room, no electric lights wasted in the summer mornings of wartime.

Hayden and I ordered breakfast in the same dining room, now illuminated with high brilliance. The waiter had no idea what Irish oatmeal was, but sliced oranges were possible. He delivered our breakfasts and the LA newspaper, and, like a married couple, we wordlessly divided it into sections and read as we ate.

I studied the book review section, a new translation of Homer, debut novels and a biography of Harding that included his sexual pecadillos. The international pages featured several photographs of angered Islamics, shaking their fists to camera with well-rehearsed rage. There was a red tide of poisonous kelp moving up the coast, now passing the southern beaches of Mexico, ultimately to sully the California coast. Hayden was still reading his sections of the paper when I said, "I'm going to check with the front desk about the Historical Society. I know they have their own building somewhere near here."

The clerk at the desk wrote down for me the opening hours of the Society from a list under the glass top. When I gave him a credit card to pay the hotel bill, he said, "Mr. Mattox, I have an envelope for you. Delivered by hand here a few hours ago."

There was only a white card in the envelope, just large enough for the bold handwriting, slanting backwards in black India ink.

Mattox
Last night my dark room
was made glorious summer by your bright sun.
Please come by before you go.
Dominic

Was I wrong to sense so early an obsessive, smothering love in Dominic, one that could trap me in a comfortable nest, unhappy or suspicious when I took a few hours off? Why couldn't I view it as a quick romp in the hay, to be forgotten before the door closes. In its way, it was not that different from the one that Hayden offered me, complete and rewarding as long as I stayed in the middle of it, basking in the overly-sweet, musky smell of loving paranoia and jealousy. You can have my body, Mattox, but you must pay the price; the castle gates are locked.

Why was I attracting this type of man? Possessive and demanding. Richard was not that way, ours was a life together where he left me annually for a seven-month sojourn in India. Albeit, it was a relationship reached only over long rocky lanes, difficult periods of adjustment. Or had the filters of my mind, the ones that delete the detritus and unsuitable ideas, strained out those occasions of jealousy and discontent?

Maybe there was not an aura over my head, but instead the aroma of need, of wanting to be loved, that I exuded like a pheromone, pulling over-excited butterflies from the depths of the rain-forest, maddened to mate, to claim ownership. I thought mental health was leaving me, *Hygeia* departing leisurely from the shore with an amused backward glance and a slow, imperious wave of her hand.

At the table, Hayden was still reading the paper. I asked him, "What is it about California? Is everybody on the make?"

"Did the desk clerk hit on you?"

"No."

"Too bad. He looked like he might when we checked in. Maybe you just need to get laid more often."

"Fair enough."

This was the last morning of our trip to Laguna and we were anxious to squeeze out every minute of joy before the mid-afternoon checkout time. A few hours on the beach and I knew that I should have slathered on more sun-block, the pink growing to an Alizarin Rose at the top of my swimming trunks. We had lunch at the other hotel, the fancier one with pink stucco at the end of the beach. An elegant dining room opened onto a seaside terrace, those customers in shorts welcome to eat outside under umbrellas. The subject of our wake-up activities was not brought up over the club sandwiches and white wine.

The Historical Society offices were in a gray-shingled house, the desk clerk had said, an easy walk from downtown. The two rooms of displays included enlarged, grainy photographs of the painters at work, most wearing linen suits, ties and black-and-white shoes. The easels weighted down by rocks on ropes under the groves of trees, leaves out of focus in the wind, women in white dresses with white umbrellas waiting together nearby. The painters painted, the companions chatted.

I searched for Simon or Latraviata in the photos, but I did not recognize any of my grandmother's artist friends. I bought a book entitled *Artistic Laguna*, including a photograph taken in the middle of a winter storm, the high waves crashing but blurred in the slower shutter speed of that time. Another book was a collection of paintings from the same years, full-page color reproductions of the sylvan, utopian scenes and small photographs of the painters who painted them. Neither Simon nor Latraviata were included. Were their lives and loves recorded only in my mind, the eager young boy who now remembered the minor Titans? Did time only remember the major painters, the ones with reputation? I thought of the woman in Santa Fe who wanted to mount an exhibit at her gallery entitled "Minor Homosexual Painters of the Upper Rio Grande in the Late Twentieth Century." Otherwise the minor ones would be erased and forgotten, she said.

Hayden and I both wanted to take a nap before leaving for Glitter Bay, so we retreated to the room, where order had been restored by the maid. The bed felt soft and welcoming as I laid down on it, a short doze almost a certainty.

Hayden put his hand on my arm and said, "About this morning. I don't fuck with men, usually, but you were different. I've been trying to figure it out."

"What do you think?"

"I want to do it again. Soon."

"Why? You're a straight man who just fell off the road a bit. It might even qualify as your mission of mercy, your good deed for the disadvantaged, to make me happy, which it did."

"It was more than that. I did have sex with my school buds back in high school, like most young guys. Locker room bumping after football. We all went back to women, some got married, and none of us talk about it today."

"I can understand that."

"But, I never got the hang of being with a woman, living with her, much less asking her to marry me. All of the women I lived with moved out on me, most of them secretly without a note while I was at work. I never knew what I did wrong or right."

"Living with men can be a different sort of difficult, Hayden. I enjoyed our sex, too, but we'll see about doing it again. I liked it a lot. It was great. I might get used to it."

I wanted to have Hayden's body again, too, to get used to it. What a delight to have those pulsing shivers that come from being next to his body, week after week. In time, I knew that a high payment, an emotional mortgage with usurious interest, would come due. Why was I so fearful of loving again? Love should not cost so much.

We slept about half an hour, then packed up the car for the return to Glitter Bay. There was no parking space near Dominic's restaurant, so Hayden offered to wait in front on the shoulder with emergency lights blinking while I went in.

Dominic was at the front desk, in shorts, a short-sleeved silk shirt and Italian black loafers again all in black. He wisely knew that black suited him, giving him a presence and stature that other Laguna residents lacked, in their pastel beach-wear. I sat down in the chair beside him and said, "We're leaving now, Dominic. I enjoyed meeting you a lot, and wish I could stay." I put my hand on his knee.

"Why don't you? I could drive you back in a couple of days. You know, I have a separate guest house, actually an old studio that belonged to one of the painters of long ago. I converted it so friends can stay there. I wouldn't bother you,...much."

"I will come back to take you up on that guest house. Late August?"

I wondered if I should kiss Dominic. He was not making any moves in that direction, so I decided to do it myself. I kissed him on the mouth just like Axton kissed me in Palm Springs, my hand pulling the back of his head towards me. I felt with my other hand his swimmer's muscles. He had the sort of body that Wilfred called all bones and peter. He was oddly compliant, giving in to my advance, unlike the aura of authority that he projected with so much thought.

He said, "Make it early August, rather than later. I'll keep a bed ready for you, Mattox. Let me know when."

"I will."

He put his arm around me on the walk to the door and stood watching while I went to the double-parked car. He leaned down to see Hayden in the driver's seat. Hayden, without enthusiasm, gave a thumbs-up in recognition.

As we left Laguna along the coast road, Hayden said, "Do you think Dominic is good-looking?"

"Yes, in a Mediterranean sort of way. Dark hair and swarthy skin tone."

"Do you think he is better-looking than me?"

"No, Hayden. As you know, your looks really turn me on. I am a lucky man."

He said, "He wants you, you know. I can see it in his eyes."

"I still like your looks better. I like you better."

We had four hours to drive and a sullen Hayden would not make it an easy trip. It was not entirely an untruth, because Hayden did continue to open hidden veins of sensuality in me, veins that had been closed since the events in Barbados.

"Good, because I like it when I know you belong to me."

Here again, somebody wanting to own me, to be Alpha male to my Beta. I naturally chose the Alpha role myself, but always looked for a partner, an equal, not one above, another below. 'Being equals' was a hard arrangement to maintain, the role of partners, mates, because it kept dissolving into the one who kissed and the one who offered the cheek. Was that Alpha/Beta really the natural way? Did each person have to decide to be active or passive, top or bottom, couldn't the night itself decide?

I said, "You know, I like the idea of a partnership better."

·100

"Okay, a partner, then. Whatever it is, you give me a hard-on knowing that you're my friend. My sexy novelist. Who would have thought I would have the hots for an intellectual writer who's so great in bed?"

I put my hand on his arm and said, "I'm going to close my eyes, now. If you get tired and want me to drive for a while, wake me up."

"I'm doing fine."

I would not be able to actually sleep, but with my eyes shut I could organize my thoughts about the week-end, make some sense. I considered with some amusement Laura's advice to uncover the underlying sexuality in my book, to have it there instead of not there. A trapdoor had opened this week-end, letting new forces out into the open and they did not want to be held back. Why, exactly, did Pandora open her box? Was it on the advice of her literary agent, something written in the margins of a first draft?

16

Newly-Caught Octopus

It was Monday morning. Hayden had left earlier for the power plant and I emerged in a haze from the week-end, made a pot of coffee. I took the cup out onto the terrace, sat in one of the canvas chairs and listened to the muffled crash of the surf through the mist. I could barely see across the beach through the fog to the water, the whiteness pressing down with a morning diligence. Remembering the loneliness of the Laguna boyhood, it filled me with the sadness. Others may want me, lust for me, but it was a temporary attraction only, dissolving in time to leave me just like this, a solitary chair on a deserted beach.

Pull yourself up, Mattox. Perhaps what I needed was to talk to people, people who knew me. I would make some calls. One agreeable aspect of living in California was that every other time zone in the nation was ahead of you and you could call eastwards without worry of waking someone. Wilfred would be up and at his writing desk.

"Is that you, Mattox? I've almost forgotten your voice," he answered.

"How are you?"

"More important, what has happened to you? I sense trouble."

"I think that is so, alas."

"Why 'alas'?"

"The trouble is the straight man that I rent the room from."

"The oh-so-straight Cordon Bleu cook? Have you bent him to your will? Tell me more."

"We had a hot time in Laguna. He came on to me, just like I thought that I wanted."

"And you didn't?"

"Not really. It was so good to have sex again, but the prospects for anything more, like a long-lasting rewarding time together are dim."

"Maybe the problem is your looking for something long-lasting. California is full of hot-patooties, buffed boys on the make. They are a natural resource like the redwoods and the beaches. One night stands. Three-days of love and goodbye. Aren't there any fags in Glitter Bay? "

"No. No self-respecting fairy would live this close to the nuclear reactor."

Wilfred clucked a bit, amused. "Our Mattox has gotten himself into a predicament again, it would seem. You may have to pull up stakes, leave your blue-collar stud and retreat to Santa Barbara."

"It's not that I don't like Hayden, he's very handsome and an accomplished lover, but I think that I hear the squeaky doors of a trap. An emotional trap. What exactly does the word 'cloy' mean?"

"To choke, clog or fill up with excess."

"Then that is what is happening to me."

"A love slave, choked with pleasure. How humorous."

"I can see the humor, too, but it doesn't lessen the problem."

"Let's move on, then, because nothing I say can help you. You'll solve it with the next time you get laid. How is your work on the book going?"

"Until now, really well. If there's trouble on the love front, the writing front is going ahead."

"Maybe you should come home. I could put together a welcome home party at Santacafe in a flash, to make a fuss over you and nurture you," he said. I thought how it would be to go back and open up the studio, to move into that old, thick-walled space. The Taos bed was perfectly comfortable for sleeping, especially for the remainder of the summer. Olivia Montelle would not be a problem, as her house was separate from the studio, a high garden wall between. I could go back, regain my sanctuary.

Wilfred continued, "Or you could go to Palm Springs and stay with

Bob Dermott. If he's gone to the cool hills of Oregon, I am sure he would let you stay there, anyway." The desert would be a hundred and twenty each day, and even the water in the Olympic pool would be too warm for comfort. Axton and his nights of paradise might be more cloying than Hayden. I would be no better off in Laguna, with Dominic weaving his black-shirted web of love, waiting for him at the bar until closing hours.

I said without conviction, "Well, thanks for listening. I guess I'll stick it out here."

"If you decide to stay, simply relax, Mattox. Don't think about where it will lead, enjoy it."

"You're right. I'll call again soon." Wilfred had a practical sense about him, despite his flamboyance.

I dialed Olivia's number to see how Ben was, how the garden looked. No answer. Laura would definitely be at her desk in New York. I filled up my coffee cup again and walked back to the terrace, the oppressive fog starting to thin, the surf not so muffled. I dialed her number.

She answered with a business-like, "Laura."

"It's Mattox."

"Oh, good, I received your signed contract and we're all set with KableOne. Regarding that, David Roth wants you to call. He is trying to set up a meeting with the staff scriptwriters. Just an idea session, he says."

"When?"

"They are on a fast track, he said, so later this week. You could drive down for the day."

"How about Thursday? Can you be there, too?"

"No, dear, this is your time to dance. I see it as a mostly ceremonial meeting, as the writers have already started work on your stories. I'll set it up. When can I see another draft of the novel? I've drummed up interest in it, on the basis of the story collection and, particularly, the sale to KableOne. Two editors want it see it, as soon as you let me see it."

"It is nearing the end. I'm starting on the last chapters today. I can send it off soon. I think that I'm moving beyond the problems."

"I'm sure you are. One of your best qualities, Mattox, is the ability to absorb advice and turn it into good writing. Many writers don't have that."

While I was talking on the phone, the fog was lifting. First glimmers of sunshine sparkled off the water and a warm breeze started softly around the corners of the cottage. I tried a call to Dominic with no answer.

I thought it must be the dark of the moon. Richard and I had paid attention to the lunar phases, both appreciating the mood altering qualities of the dark phase, asking each other if this was the day or was it tomorrow? I feel so bad now, the dark must be today, he would say.

I knew that my grief for Richard was there still, the strange neighbor who constantly peered out of her window, black eyes glistening behind the lace curtains. Did this lament really go away in time, on its own, a threnody moving farther and farther away until not a single note could be heard? I had the unhappy notion that I would hear more passages of it.

As the sun broke through, I thought of the shady circle where they pulled Richard's body from the sea, his limp hand still feeling warm in mine. Time turned to hours as I sat holding him, friends standing silent in a worried circle, helpless to relieve him or lessen the numb cloud over me. Don't dust the sand off his face, the policeman warned me, the coroner must see him as he was. Richard was a man, when alive, who spent hours in front of the mirror, getting the hair just right, changing shirts six times before going out, checking closely each day for crows-feet. What had happened at sea to bring this about, this shroud of sand?

If sorrow did not slink away of its own volition, it needed to be trampled, to be flattened until no part of it moved. I saw the image of the Mykonos fisherman who whacked the newly-caught octopus on the rocks in front of the tavernas, slapping it over his head onto the granite wharf, again and again. To make sure it was dead and its long strands softened. You must murder grief that way, smash it into oblivion, as dead as Richard himself was.

I could see how the women in black all over the world savored, keening and crying, the continual presence of death, an ever-present sister, giving comfort with her ready vocabulary of soothing words. Time will heal you, sister. He was a good man, sister. Give in to the tears. What good years they were before he went, sister. There was a comfort in such memory, in the consoling breezes from beyond the river.

But here, on this day, I knew there was in front of me a frontier between that old life and a new one. A dotted line on the beach. The life yet-to-come beckoned with attractive fingers, sensual fingers, scaring me. Step across it, Mattox, and move on. Do not live just to honor death. Come dance the dance. Step across.

17

Joshua, Hallelujah

I did not get much writing done in the two days following our week-end in Laguna, thoughts of past and present turning around like dust devils. There was only a day left before my meeting with David Roth and his crew of scriptwriters. When he left for the day, Hayden asked me to keep an eye on the low-temperature pot cooking a roast. He would finish up the meal when he got back from work.

I walked for more hours than usual, rounding the point to the south, along the un-cottaged beach, Pearly Gates, and around the next promontory beyond. The tide was low enough for me to run around the end rocks between waves, reaching dry land as the water crashed up against the cliff.

The third beach, beyond, was also pristine, a smaller cove protected by a reef-like crescent of rocks, with clear, still waters near shore. I had promised Hayden I would not swim alone, but there was no chance of rip-tide or undertow in this calm haven. Shedding my shorts, I walked slowly into the pool.

I pulled in my breath with shock as I dived under the surface, aware of the bundled thoughts that came rushing up in response. The cold waters jolted the past from its hiding place, memories of events three years ago, when I walked into another, warmer sea.

It was September in Barbados, the year before Richard's death. He and I had arrived on a late flight from Miami and the drive to the rental villa on the West Coast was entirely in the dark, a lurching taxi driven by a kindly old man with glasses a half-inch thick. He drove in the exact center of the road, the painted line in the roadway aligned with the hood ornament, and we were often blinded by the lights of the oncoming cars, which honked and swerved.

He was very proud to find the secluded cottage in the dark, down an unmarked drive lined by mahogany trees, each with eye-level rings of orchids around the trunks. The caretaker had waited for us, and she opened the closed house. As she unlatched the line of shutters, she said that the cook, Magritta, would arrive at ten the next morning. She asked if we were going right to sleep, tired from our trip.

"No," Richard said, "we want a swim in the sea before sleep, to change our ions." We looked over the front terrace to the lapping waters, dimly lit by a single spotlight in an overhanging tree. In our trunks in a few minutes, we raced down the steps to the beach and into the tepid waters of the Caribbean. Joy and new negative ions.

It was a last-minute trip, Richard just back from India to be with me on my birthday, before going back to the monastery in the foothills of the Himalayas. He was in the middle of a Ngondra practice, a million prostrations required, but he took a break to join me. I don't know how many more of your birthdays we can be together, he said. You can write your stories, I can work on my Tibetan.

The swim refreshed us after the five hour flight. We mixed a rum punch from the small store provided by the estate agents and sat to dry ourselves on the terrace, the cadence from the tree frogs an almost-steady shriek.

The two-week stay was an idyll, perhaps discounted by the unexpectedly high heat and the afternoon rainstorms that pelted the house for hours. Most unusual, the neighbors in adjoining villas insisted, September could be counted upon for fair afternoons and cooling trade winds. Despite the storms, Richard studied and wrote his Sanskrit-like prayers, while I put a polish on three stories with dips into the plunge-pool to keep cool.

The cook, Magritta, and her helper, a very thin, curiously uncoordinated black girl named Penelope, did not know what to make of us in the morning. An older man with his young lover, how were they supposed to react? How long had we known each other? Over ten years now. Oh, well, then. Would it be a great inconvenience to provide a separate vegetarian meal for Richard? No direct answer, some mumbling, no smiles.

All of the cottages came with a cook and a house maid. This cottage, Seaside, was one of the smaller offered, its setting right on the sea with steps down to the water and it had seemed at booking time a better choice than the ones farther back, with a kitchens separate from the dining rooms.

We ate our meals at a small table with the two women watching from the immediately adjacent work area. After several days, the awkwardness was only slightly lessened by our getting accustomed to the women being there, looking without emotion at every bite. Richard told me he was going to do something about it.

While we were waiting for Magritta to sautée the flying fish she had bought at the market that morning, Richard asked Penelope if he could read her hand. She giggled and looked down.

Could he really read people's hands? Margitta watched with a sharp eye from the stove as Richard talked and turned Penelope's hand over, inspecting even between the fingers.

I had always discounted Richard's palmistry, assuming it was an unfortunate adjunct to his Buddhist studies, a vanity that students of Eastern knowledge imagined they could see what we Westerners could not. But with Penelope, from the outset Richard got to the very real matters of her life. I've forgotten the details exactly, but she had lost a sister, broken a leg falling from a tree as a girl, been abandoned by her man in the night (another would find her soon), and she had one child, a small boy. There was more, particular places where she traveled when young, Trinidad and St. Vincent, and storms that she had survived.

Penelope was stunned. I, always the cynic, felt that it was surely mere fakery. I reckoned that most Barbados women had a departed man and a child, with even odds of its being a boy, so Richard's chances of being mostly right were better than good. Trinidad and St. Vincent were the only places nearby to go. Magritta looked clouded as she watched on.

The reading was cut off as the dinner was ready, Penelope serving with a bit more punctilio and Magritta watching in a somewhat less dour gaze from the kitchen. As the women washed up before they left for the night, Penelope asked if she could bring her son for a reading tomorrow. He was fourteen months, a good, quiet boy. He would not stay long. Richard assented.

The next day, before the boy's hand could be read, Magritta asked Richard if he will look at her hand first. She was, after all, in charge of Seaside Cottage. Lunch was waiting, but since it was to be all cold food, a salad for Richard and lobster morsels for me, nothing would be ruined.

He studied her palm, bigger and more sharply angled than Penelope's, doing the same preparatory steps of turning it over and looking between the fingers. He found in it personal, particular information, different from last night's, facts that delighted Magritta as much as Penelope, who held her chubby, solemn son so he could watch the proceedings. Two cousins, whose presence had not been approved or even discussed last night, looked over the kitchen counter with wide eyes. This small crowd was visibly impressed with Richard, this Englishman who read those strange Tibetan books on the night table. Magritta stood aside with arms crossed to watch the reading of the boy's small hand. Richard gently pried open his fingers from a closed fist.

He said, after the initial inspection process, "He has a long life line, no break or waver in it at all. Ninety good years. He will be happy and healthy." Penelope nodded and said that he never had colds like other children, seldom cried. Richard continued, "Also, this cross here on the heart line says he will be a great holy man and people will sing his praises."

I wondered if Richard had overstepped in the embellishment department. Nothing went to the head like necromancy, but Penelope looked even more astonished, happier than the last night.

She told us that their preacher, just last month, in front of the whole

Ebeneezer Church, refused to christen the boy under her chosen name of Henry Allen, her father's name, but renamed him on the spot Joshua, proclaiming the boy had great future as one of Barbados's new preachers. He could rid the island entirely of Satan. The church, Penelope said, broke into song the likes of which had not been heard in years, hallelujahs could be heard all the way into Holetown, the kicking but happy Joshua held high.

Richard had seen all that in the hand of that grave-expressioned boy. In our remaining days in Barbados, we saw something bordering on adoration radiating from the kitchen, no vegetarian dish too difficult, no open-air market too distant. The cousins found extra root vegetables and lettuces in their gardens and the fruit basket on the counter stood high with mangos of several colors, short purple bananas and passion fruit. Richard's glass at the table was never empty and extra servings came without their being asked for. I, although recognized as simply the disbelieving companion, the infidel, was bathed in the same veneration.

Magritta pulled me aside one day to tell me that I must look over Richard, guard him closely, because he was a holy man, himself, a shaman. To see like he did was a Gift. *Don't you let nothing happen to him.* That night in bed after the lights were out, I asked Richard if the holy man was ready to get laid, to know the heavenly joy. He did not think I was particularly funny, but agreed.

A few days later, while we swam, he said, "It's unfair, you know."

"What?"

"I study and study for enlightenment. It is so slow, so hard."

"I admire that, Richard, you know I do. I see a difference in you since you've started your Tibetan work. You're a wiser, better man." We were treading water in an area where the bottom was sandy, our shadows clear on the rippled sand.

"But you've had it all along, like your blue eyes and artistic hands. You were just born with it. A mystical enlightenment."

"I don't know that that's so."

111

"I do. You told me about the *kundalini* that you can make go up your spine. The yoga master tried to explain it to us at the monastery, but nobody got it, nobody could make it happen. You can release it without effort in the middle of an afternoon nap, no appreciation at all of how difficult it is."

"I'm not sure it's really *kundalini*, perhaps only a ripple of some built-in energy."

"Take if from me, it *is* real. I'm a failure."

Richard was getting too serious as he often did, too unhappy with himself. I said, "But I am a failure, too, because I keep trying to levitate like your rinpoches during those naps...only a few inches off the cushions. But nothing."

"And, see, you mock me. It's really not fair."

"Lighten up, I'm not mocking you."

"At least I can swim better than you." He coursed off at high speed straight out to sea, a fast breast-stroke that brought his head bobbing up again and again, his thick black hair shiny as an otter's.

I turned to continue my slow side-stroke parallel to the shore, in front of Oliver Messel's former villa, the elegant coral steps leading right down into the sea-water. It was as if he expected attractive luncheon guests to arrive from under the sea, dropping pieces of kelp and barnacles as they made their way up to his silver and crystal laden table.

In intriguing ways, Richard and Hayden were similar. Simple personalities that reacted immediately without thought to stimuli, not the many-layered consideration that preceded any action from me. Richard was smarter than Hayden, more talented; but Hayden did not have the black torment that colored part of every day for Richard. They were both very physical, loving sports, competition, games that jostled you about. I remembered Hayden after his half hour with the volleyball group in Laguna, and Richard after a steep run in the foothills of Santa Fe, both with dilated eyes, bubbling with an excitement and happiness that nothing cerebral offered. They could have been brothers.

A tarot reader in Santa Fe, a fat woman at the Psychic Faire with noisy bracelets and eyes that missed little in the real world, said that I was an Old Person, a category she clearly respected. Richard looked on impassively.

I had endured many, many former lives, she said, with all the sad experience and disillusion that those lives afford, like the battered tree trunk of an ancient oak. Richard, she said, observing his great beauty, enormous sex appeal and earnest wish to be multi-leveled, was not. This was his first life. She had no explanation for this dilemma, eyes never glancing my way but completely focused on Richard's perfect profile.

Hayden and Richard were clearly, then, New People, with no reincarnated bank accounts to call upon, no pre-knowledge of the human condition, nothing pre-wired to give them direction. Were all handsome people that way? It was not without irony that the old gods pre-ordained that the New and Old were to live together, to be attracted to each other, like the Cold and the Hot, the Tall and the Short, the Prince and the Pauper. And just how had this expert palmist and incipient monk, who knew the secrets, meet and stay with this Old One, who seemed to know nothing? Why did I even listen to all this reincarnation babble?

Back in the clear, cold waters of the California cove, I could hear Magritta's words of warning. *Don't you let nothing happen to him.* I knew that I had let something happen to him. I had been charged with looking out for, guarding Richard by a matron sister of the Ebeneezer Christ Church of Barbados, and I let down my watch, let Richard drown in calm waters. Was it Palinurus who did the same, not paying attention to the course of his ship, letting his fellow sailors die in a shipwreck? As I swam back to shore, I knew that guilt, even some of it metaphysical or paranormal, was one of the engines that kept my grief alive.

18

Broken Circle

Garnet beckoned to me from her terrace as I walked along the beach, back from my still-water swim. She had her tea pot and cups ready, as if expecting me. I supposed she had seen me walking south, knew I was soon to return and wanted the news of our Laguna trip. Garnet did not miss much of the comings and goings along her beach. I kissed her tanned, wrinkled cheek and sat down.

"Where did you stay?" she asked.

"The old hotel on the beach," I said, "El Desirio"

"Did you share a room?"

"We even shared a bed. That's all they had, king-sized beds."

Garnet smiled as she looked over at me. "Hayden has the ability to delight, doesn't he?"

She would not be put aside, I was sure, by avoiding the issue. "More than delight, Garnet, he's an amazing lover. We had quite a time. I'm still not sure what it means. It happened so naturally, so without planning."

"Let him love you, Mattox. It's what he's good at. I used to call him my love machine, and he was quite proud of that."

I laughed, "That's what my friend Wilfred advised me."

"Do, because there aren't really many good lovers in this world. When one like Hayden takes a fancy to you, it's like you've pulled the golden ring."

"He said he wanted to do it again, and again. Soon."

"Let him, because it's the gift he is proud to give and he knows it is of the best quality. One fine day he'll move on, like he always does."

114

Without looking directly at Garnet, I said, "Did you have a sexual affair with Hayden, too?"

"I was too old for real sex, even then, but he knew how to taunt me. An old woman's drive is still there, only creaky, hard to get going. He gave me what passes for sex at my age and I called him my dance-away lover. That was a number of years ago when I really looked a lot younger and was not ashamed of my inner thigh."

I did not want any more details, but Garnet's lack of suspicion and jealousy was refreshing. I could see why Hayden liked her so much. She took on matters of sex, the heart, and potential disloyalty without emotion. Did her years behind the camera give her that, the ability to look at love as a performance, a part of the screen-play to be marked by the script-girl as "Scene 23, Fourteen Takes, Done?" I felt that her candor was not without heart, however; she could look upon Hayden with a sweet objectivity.

There was in me the shred of a thought that Hayden might not move on from his fascination with me; to stay fixated on me, unlike those that went before. Hubris in its full, horrid bloom. I would be dealing with Hayden for years to come. How might Garnet take to that? It was okay if Hayden played the field, changed partners, made his well-lubricated machine do its work, but how would it be if he focused only on one person, me? What if he settled down, as they say? I better keep that thought in my own head, not spoken out over Garnet's tea table.

I said, instead, "I wonder how much he's looking for his father again. I know it's not natural to go to bed with your father, but it all mixes up in his mind. Love and loss, thrown together like marble cake. I am what he didn't have, or I represent it in his mind."

"He's still not over his father's death, I know, and his mother turned her back on him. It meant a broken family, a broken circle. If he loved his sister, his uncle, even physically loved them, strong enough, he could make it whole, mend it. If he's good enough at it, maybe the family would function again. I think Hayden has made you a part of his cracked-open family, another member to try his considerable skill upon."

"Curious as that sounds, I know you're right, Garnet."

"Don't let yourself get hurt, because the machine will decide to drive away one day."

"We are both already hurt, in my mind." What's going to happen is clear, like a long road unwavering to its destination across the desert. Hayden will not depart. It will be me who departs, another abandonment, only intensifying his need to hold on. "It's inevitable. I think about things too much."

"That's why you're a writer, I suspect."

We sat in silence for a while and it felt comfortable, good. The wind along the beach was picking up, the sound of the breakers more of a crash than a murmur. Garnet did not interrupt with unnecessary chatter, something she definitely learned on the demanded quiet of the movie set. She reached across, took my hand in hers and we sat watching the sea. It was enjoyable to be hand-in-hand with Garnet, both of us Hayden's beloveds. It was somehow like touching Hayden.

When I left, I asked, "May I come back again?"

She nodded, "Always, Mattox."

As I walked back up the beach, I made a mental note to find a time to ask Hayden if he and Ambrose had sex together. I was sure Garnet and Sylvan both had, and I wondered about Henry Clarence, another father to conquer. It may be what everybody on Glitter Bay had in common, a time in the sack with Hayden, for some a longer time than others. I was just the latest to be there.

19

Chinese Bowls

At dinner that night with Hayden and Ambrose, Sylvan asked the same question about the Laguna sojourn, "Where did you stay?"

I wanted the line of my answers to take a different course than those with Garnet. Sylvan's interest in our activities in bed might not have the older woman's kind regard. Roles were changing; I thought in the past weeks that I saw Sylvan turning from my proponent to my adversary, Hayden from an innocent conspirator to a guilty one.

"The old hotel on the beach," I said. "El Desirio?"

"Did you share a room?" Unhappily, the answers were taking the same course.

I said, "We did. A double with a great view of the sea from the balcony." Hayden looked across at me with interest, but did not enter in the talk.

Sylvan kept on. "What did you do?"

"We went swimming, looked around at the shops and galleries, walked up to my grandmother's old cottage, had a late dinner at Dominic's on the main drag, a great steak and seafood place. Hayden met a nice girl at the bar."

Sylvan looked over at Hayden. "I expect you had to ball her?"

Hayden said, "It's been a long time, Syl, and the sex was good." Did she notice him look across at me as he spoke that last bit? I thought about Garnet's assessment of Hayden's machine-like abilities. Was Sylvan missing those? Did he in fact walk away from her like Garnet said?

She said, "What was her name?"

"I don't remember. Do you, Mattox?"

I shook my head. Sylvan continued, "It doesn't sound serious, then."

Hayden said, "No. A quickie. I came back to the hotel about midnight, woke up Mattox even though I tried to be quiet."

Sylvan appeared to have a premonition that her monopoly on Hayden's love was in harm's way. She would not rest until more of the truth was known. The hunt was on.

"Just one night for so much love," she said

Ambrose said, "Let's raise the level of our conversation a little. Mattox, did you find what you were looking for in Laguna? And I haven't seen you since your research trip to Pasadena. How's it going, the book and the delving into the past?"

"Well on all fronts, Ambrose. The book has the working title of *Imperial Yellow*. I'm using a Chinese bowl as a symbol in my grandmother's life; she was attracted to a Chinese man from afar, a love affair of the mind."

"I like the sounds of it. Will you let me read it? Before you mail it off to the publishers?"

"If you like. I'm always awkward with that, because you might expect too much."

"I'll just check for misspellings, poor diction, and run-on sentences like I do for my students. The grand course of your narrative I'll leave up to you."

"Okay, then. I'll print out a copy for you this week. It may all seem like one run-on sentence."

"I doubt it."

"The yellow bowl is the last bit of research I need. There are antique stores in Chinatown and Beverly Hills that sell high-end, museum quality porcelains. I want to see them in person, and ask the store-owners some questions."

Ambrose said, "I saw Chinese bowls in the Topkapi in Istanbul. Big yellow bowls, a bright, brownish yellow, in the glass cases of the porcelain museum. I thought they were just kitchen bowls, to mix pancake batter for the Ottomans. Are they valuable?"

I said, "I think very. I'll tell you exactly how valuable after I talk to those old Chinese merchants. It's important to my story that they have high value now, and a commensurate one thirty years ago, adjusting for currency values. In one chapter, grandmother sells the yellow bowl for us to live on after the banks go bust."

"I read about a recent auction of Chinese items in New York. I think they brought record prices. Ming Dynasty or Tang Dynasty, I don't remember."

Hayden felt left out, wanting in. He said, "Can I go on that trip, too?" I told him that I would save the yellow bowls for a week-end when we could both go, maybe this next one? His worried brow unfurrowed, relaxed.

When I looked over at Sylvan, she returned my glance with an interested, long gaze. I thought she suspected that Hayden and I had bonded in some way. Perhaps she had misread me, ignored the danger that I now displayed. Ambrose's well-bred detour around her searching operation had not ended the quest, I felt sure.

Your brother and I had a hot night together; correction, a hot morning of frottage. That's not French for cheese, Sylvan. The book-writer, all sweetness and light from the beginning, trapped your brother in his sticky web, your innocent, sensual sibling that you counted upon as your own, the one you consoled when girlfriends abandoned.

She could be reading my mind, the unconcealed message on my forehead that I had made love with her brother, when she said, "Let get back to what happened in Laguna."

Hayden entered in with, "It's great there, Syl. Lot's more to do than Glitter Bay."

"I'll bet. Were there a lot of gay guys around?"

"We didn't see many. Maybe that desk clerk at the hotel. He hit on you, didn't he, Mattox?"

I said, "Maybe. I'm usually too dumb to recognize when I've been hit on."

"Dominic seemed to pay you a lot of attention, too."

"Now that was a hit and I recognized it."

Sylvan said, "I don't think you're dumb at all, Mattox. Maybe you should write your book down in Laguna. They all seem to want you there."

"I feel wanted here, too." It was a weak parry and I could expect more sharp blades.

"But more down there in Laguna."

Ambrose saw that his simple diverting tactics would not work, so he said, "Sylvan, Mattox is a welcome addition to our family. Stop pestering him."

She said, "All right."

Ambrose forcibly turned the talk to innocuous matters and kept it there. When he was in the house, his brother's children relented. He asked me polite questions about book writing in general, who really read in today's world, what publishers were looking for, and were there any messages in writing today. He expertly hogged the conversation until the last slice of roast was gone, dessert finished, coffees drunk, directing questions only to me, and totally ignoring Hayden and Sylvan.

She more than once looked over at me with a blank expression, one that I expected hid a meaner one below. She would not rebel against her uncle, but bide her time for a battle with me later. It might be difficult for me to avoid a one-on-one confrontation with Sylvan before the end of summer. I felt a sympathy for her; I did not want to make her sad. I could understand her love of Hayden, her compulsion.

She left first, kissing Ambrose and Hayden, smiling over at me. We sat at the dining table while Ambrose talked about affairs at the college. Hayden was the dutiful son, asking questions about every topic, listening intently to Ambrose's academic information.

After Hayden cleared the table and worked at the kitchen chores, Ambrose turned to me and said, "Mattox, you've become a good friend for Hayden. He sorely needs a stabilizer in his life, a rudder if you will."

"I'm not certain that I can offer him that," I said.

"Hayden will not admit to it, pride one of his few failings, but I can see it, well enough. He's adrift, wants direction, someone to love."

"I am sure that it was a compliment, Ambrose, that I could give Hayden a center. But I doubt that I can."

"About Sylvan. Don't let her suspicions upset you; she always rebelled against Hayden's friends. She's deathly afraid of losing her brother."

I knew she was afraid of losing more than a brother, a secret lover whose body could make her shiver with desire. Garnet had several times implied that there was more there than sibling regard, even now. Sylvan thought that when she brought me into Hayden's house that I was safely outside of his sensual purview, no competition possible from a gay man. Now, some small sensual signal had alerted her otherwise. Siblings sometimes knew such things. I felt sorry for Sylvan, the strongest tie in her life was unraveling.

I suspected that Hayden and Richard had another quality in common, the inability to have a friend or associate without turning them into a sexual object. Richard had found the foothills of the Himalayas a rich source for his dalliances, but far enough away from me in distance and spirit to avoid any dangers to our Santa Fe home together. Hayden had turned me, as I am sure he did his uncle and sister, in earlier days, but as Garnet observed, the machine moved on.

I answered Ambrose, "I'm not upset with Sylvan. After all, she was the one who brought me here."

He left us and I helped Hayden in the kitchen. I watched him, standing straight like a marine. He washed while I dried, placing the dishes back on the shelves. It was oddly domestic, somehow proper, definitely comfortable.

As I said goodnight and went to leave, Hayden reached over for my arm. "I was watching you at dinner. Can I come to your bed tonight?" I told him that I would like that, and he did come.

20

The Boiler Room

Hayden had already left the bed, an hour earlier than usual, when I awoke. It was the day for my drive into Burbank and the meeting with the scriptwriters. I had not found a time to tell Hayden that I was going south for the day, and I was anxious for no repeat performance about my abandoning him. I left a note on the counter explaining the trip, promising that I would be back sometime in the evening. He should eat alone, but I would be there in time for a cup of espresso and to tell him what happened.

Before leaving, I called Wilfred. He would want to know about my day with the script-writers.

"I have news, Wilfred."

"Tell me quick."

"I'm heading south in five minutes to Hollywood... Burbank actually. To talk to the writers who are converting my stories to scripts."

"What are you wearing?"

"Jeans, a white shirt, sneakers." Costume was important to Wilfred.

"No, no, no."

"Why?"

"We can't have you looking like Willie off the pickle ship. No way."

"So what must I wear?"

"Your chinos, you look thinner in those, a dark cotton shirt, black or dark blue is best, and those black Italian loafers we bought you on the cruise last winter. No socks."

"All that is possible."

"Then, you might have a chance of meeting someone new, turn a head or two. Jeans and sneakers don't cut it in Tinsel Town."

Wilfred knew the nuances of dress better than I did, so I hung up and did what he said. It was a three hour drive to the KableOne offices, a faux-adobe complex with touches of Santa Fe Style, applied vigas projecting out of each wall. I parked in the adjoining parking lot just at eleven o'clock and walked into the reception area, a high-ceilinged space, rustic ceiling beams and a corner fireplace with an oval-arched firebox. The receptionist was blonde, very pretty with a well-bred English voice.

"I'll just tell David that you're here."

I had learned somewhere that, in Hollywood offices, British girls with Oxbridge accents were eagerly sought for the front desk, where they gave an elegant façade to the workings in the back rooms. While she answered the phone with her clipped tones, I looked at the display behind her. Enlarged photographs of scenes from the network's programs lined the wall, sit-coms with titles that I did not recognize and many nature shows with names that I did, *Days with the Lions. Whale! Whale!* and *Go Flamingo Go.*

I remembered David Roth, back in our schooldays, as the boy who was terrified of birds, falling flat on the ground when a mockingbird swooped near; I saw him once tip-toe across the street to avoid a toothless sleeping dog. Nature was big on KableOne's menu, making amends for a fauna-free childhood of a scared boy with knobby knees and thick glasses.

He came out of his office with a smile, walking towards me with arms outstretched. "Mattox, how long has it been?"

"A lifetime, David." We hugged in the manly manner, no body contact whatsoever. He kept a hand on each of my arms, looked intently at me.

As Laura had observed, he was no longer skinny, but I recognized the David I knew under the well-designed glasses, the thick lenses still there, and the salon-created curly hair that might have some color added. Hadn't his father already turned white when we were boys? He was not fat, his stomach flat over a pair of red canvas trousers, but it was obvious that keeping his weight down had become a problem for David. He wore a well-tailored shirt over the trousers, and crocodile tassel-loafers. David looked what he was, a prosperous, perhaps talented, television producer. I wondered who I would have become had I stayed in California. Would I be at a desk in David's offices?

"They're all waiting in here." We walked across the foyer to another door which he opened for me. Four young people were sitting around a conference table, all in their twenties, I would guess.

"These are my young Turks. This is Brenda, here, our straw-boss, Wally's over there, Erik next to him and Patricia is at the end. Say hello to Mattox Williams, the painter turned writer."

"Hello, Mattox Williams." Like a school-room. They each had a tattered copy of my book and a pile of typewritten papers.

Brenda was the spokesperson. Sitting at the end of the table, she patted her hand on the empty chair next to her. It also had a book and a pile of typescript in front. When coffee and water were provided, everybody sat back down with David placed across from me, Brenda between us.

She radiated authority; slim, with boney arms and short hair; she had a manly air about her. I liked her right off the bat, thought my book was in good hands. There were several broad-shouldered, short-haired women in my stories, women that I liked, so maybe a sympathetic bell also rang in Brenda.

She said, "We are thrilled, of course, to be producing your stories. We think the whole world will be fascinated with the inner workings of an artist community, and Santa Fe is a beautiful place to have it all happen. Let me tell you how we have dealt with the stories. We divided them among us, each taking six stories to produce an outline, a treatment, as we call it. Some are already in script form."

David interrupted, "Mattox, our staff has written three shows together, all from story collections. Two are shooting now, one in Vancouver, another in Wyoming for Bettye Stuart's tales about the plight of the ranch-woman. She grew up on a ranch with many funny situations to tell. We know what we're doing and I think you'll be pleased. This is the team, the Turks, that every studio in town is eager to kidnap. The salary offers keep going up, I have heard."

The four writers beamed at his appreciation, but I wondered if their employ would survive the year if bonuses and raises were not forthcoming. David carefully did not reiterate that the book option contract excluded powers for me to add or detract, but instead granted the right to "confer." Laura had pointed this out to me, but we left in the clause; I did not want to try my hand at script-writing. This was a courtesy meeting, so that it could be said on the credits somewhere that the show was produced in conference with the author.

I said, "I am sure that I will be pleased." Why fight the current? It was too strong.

Brenda said, "We have incorporated most of your dialogue, changed it only if it did not sound right for the particular actors we have cast. In some of the stories, you had very little dialogue, as you know, and in those cases we have added lines in the spirit of the story. That pile of scripts in front of you is yours to keep, to look at and make comments upon. You do not have to read them today. We expect to be shooting most of the episodes in Santa Fe starting in September."

The meeting proceeded in this manner, my attendance a ceremonial performance only. We discussed the stories in general, the writers asking questions about certain of the characters, where they might find the paintings needed as props, and what qualities they might expect from what painter's studios. The agents were already at work casting the minor parts from local lists and choosing locations.

Patricia, at the end of the table in dark glasses, said, "Let me ask you about Cecily Brompton in the long story. Is she really O'Keeffe?"

"Not necessarily; there were other strong women who painted in Santa Fe, some almost as successful as O'Keeffe, but not as well known. Basically, I saw it as a story between an older woman, young in mind and spirit, and a young man who is mature beyond his years."

"Do you think there was physical love between her and Carlos?"

"Who's to say what happened late at night after dinner? The gap in their ages seems too great, but some young men find the experienced woman more attractive. Sex between them is not necessary for the story to happen." The group muttered more than laughed.

Erik asked me, "Is Magnus Morrison, the painter of the Pueblo maidens, actually you? Should we think of him as younger than you described in the story, more your age?"

"The characters are all probably me. Like Jung's assessment of dreams. In the waking world, though, I would probably have chosen to paint the Pueblo warriors, but maidens worked better for the story." This got no reaction from the group.

As the meeting went on, it was clear that lengthy answers were not expected from me, and, after a few attempts when their eyes glazed and pencils twitched, none given. I felt like the duchess on a world cruise, given a tour of the ship where she issued upper-class encouragements for the shirtless men in the depths of the boiler room, everyone anxious for her to return to an upper deck so they could get back to real work.

Before I could regain the relative safety of the deck chair, David offered an early lunch down the street, just the two of us. To catch up, he said; it was an easy walk.

We were seated in a booth upholstered in maroon leather, along a wall of identical booths in a windowless restaurant. It took a few minutes for my eyes to adjust to the gloom, the day outside bright and without smog. Burbank eateries did not like the light of day, too harsh for the television lens perhaps, too injurious to illusion.

The waiter asked for my drink order, while he delivered to David, without his asking, a large stemmed glass of white wine with ice-cubes. The return trip on the freeways awaited me, so iced tea, please, no sugar.

"What do you think, Mattox? Are you excited?"

"I'm impressed, David. The young writers are all so bright, so quick."

"You can count on their doing a good job. I was delighted with the book. Who knew you could write so well?"

"Thanks. Tell me about yourself. Are you married? Children?"

"No, on both counts. I was married right out of USC. Do you remember Marjorie Eastover?" He took a large drink from the wine glass.

"Of course. But it didn't last, then, because you're now single?"

"We split after three years. Her family was against me from the start."

"I remember the old Doctor Eastover and his wife. They did not let anybody near their dear Marjorie." For good reason, as I remember, because the secret name for her in school was Our Lady of the Blow-Jobs. It seems unkind and mean-spirited now. I suspected that David was never party to that information.

"I was little better than a mail clerk at the time, at Paramount Studios. But it was show business, if only the bottom rung." He laughed.

So the marriage of the young Marjorie and David gave them space and time to repair the scars from their thoughtless school-mates, and to go on, healed and oblivious, to the further adventures of adulthood. That ill-treatment by the young peers may be all that they had in common, vanishing as their self-esteem quotients grew. They were classic examples of early unhappiness that propelled a person into success. I wondered what high-floored office Marjorie looked out of as we talked, suited in red with a battalion of minions at her beck.

I said, "You've done very well since then."

"They call me ambitious and driven now."

"I suspect that is somewhat true. You've always held on to things like a terrier. David, I should formally thank you for being in the position to buy my book, and for actually buying it."

"Laura Grabowski says you're about finished with work on a novel. Should I look at it?"

"I doubt it could make a film; it's mostly interior thoughts, musings and ruminations of a gay man, who happens to be a painter and his early life with grandmother, who happens to be like Anna. You can do only so many voice-overs."

"You should let me be the judge. Paramount is making a movie about

Proust right now, and I would expect nothing but musings. And I hear they are filming a story about two cowboys who were lovers for decades, in Wyoming. Being gay is not a bad thing in Hollywood anymore. Send me a copy of the manuscript when it's done. I remember Anna, you know. She was always good to me."

"Thanks, I will send it to you. You know, David, you don't have to continue to buy my work just because we were friends in school."

"I'm not. I like your work." He finished off the white wine, rattled the ice and held the glass up to the waiter for another.

"I had thoughts that you might be trying to repay me, for all those fights?"

"All what fights?"

"The ones you had while we were at McKinley Elementary. The ones that I broke up."

"I don't remember any fights." This was awkward. Maybe he remembered saving me from the bullies who bloodied noses or his pulling off the pugnacious girls, anxious to give me bruises. With the return of his self-esteem came a loss of what really happened. How we get things turned around in our minds.

A sudden flash occurred to me. Was I doing the same thing in Imperial Yellow, painting a skewed picture of reality? Had Laura seen that un-verisimilitude in my book, an underlying lack of truth that all readers would also see? No, I think I got it right, but only slightly blemished in the telling, and, after all, it was fiction; where events did not need to match actual occurrences, if you could convince the reader otherwise.

It did not feel right, however, to leave his denial completely uncontested. I said, "There were a few fights, David, and I clearly recall the times when we put Anna's Cuticura salve on your cuts. But it was a long time ago."

I could also remind him of the three Beasley boys who sat on him for ten minutes, laughing, taunting; that grouchy boy with a shaved head who lived on Glenarm Street, always a skirmish waiting to happen; and Harriet

Flagg and her sister, both big for their years, quick to settle things with closed fists. Early on they mastered the painful technique of twisting arms up behind backs.

"Like an ice age ago," he said.

"The Pleistocene." I felt unctous at such disavowal, a toady to thirty thousand dollars.

"Why are you staying up in Glitter Bay? I've never known anybody who stayed there. Is it nice?"

"It suits me, David. A quiet town with a good beach, and I have a lovely work table. There's not much going on there, no distractions."

"I'll have to check it out, sometime."

"You might not like it. It lacks Hollywood's verve."

We finished our lunches and walked back to the offices. I asked David, "Tell me about the good antique shops in Beverly Hills, the ones with expensive Chinese pieces."

"They're all together on Mountolive Street, just off Melrose. Seven or eight shops, as I recall; the street is only a block long and it looks like Chinatown West. Why?"

"I have to get back today, but I'm coming down this week-end to research some things. Chinese porcelains. Hayden Danning, the man I rent from in Glitter Bay, may come with me. I guess we'll stay over near there Saturday night. I remember plenty of hotels on Melrose."

"I've got a guest house and an eighty-foot lap pool. Stay with me, I'm ten minutes from where you want to go."

David's house would be a great deal better than a seedy Art Deco motel. If I was forbidden the editing powers on the short story project, at least I could take advantage of some of the ancillary perks. Hayden might enjoy seeing behind the walls of Beverly Hills, and, for that matter, I would too.

"Are you sure?"

"No problem. Just call me when you get here, I'll be home all day." When we returned to the pueblo lobby, he asked the English girl to write down his address and unlisted cell-phone number.

"Again, thanks, David. See you Saturday."

On the trip back north, I thought about the KableOne project and what it might mean to me. None of my friends in Santa Fe watched much television, so it would neither add nor subtract from my status with them. Among them, my writing was considered a novelty, something I had oddly undertaken too late in life to make a difference, like hybridizing peonies or tap dancing. I was still a painter to them, an artist with a regional reputation, too ensconced in one world to travel far into another. Perhaps they were right. The rolling credits on the television series would pass as quickly as the fame, I was sure. From a story by Mattox Williams.

I took the coast road from Santa Barbara on, convertible top down, watching the surf as the sun dipped into redness, enjoying the full speed limit as I escaped the long grasp of the LA afternoon traffic. The sun was still up as I drove down the oyster shell driveway, the crunching sound of home.

21

Give Me the Cobra Juice

On Saturday, we went to Mountolive Street, Hayden finding the row of Chinese merchants with ease. It was about noon on Saturday, but there was a vacant parking spot with a meter, twenty five cents for each ten minutes. Hayden had a store of quarters in the ash-tray so we contracted for forty minutes, long enough, I thought, for a look into each store.

The first one specialized in furniture, altar tables of bleached sandalwood against every wall, the pale look more appreciated by West Coast decorators. The adjoining shop showed cases of precious stones and some antique jewelry, several vitrines full of smaller Canton blue and white pieces, plates and the classic pure white bowls. I saw from outside the window of the third shop a large yellow bowl on a pedestal, under protective, transparent cubes, a technique learned from museums.

"Are you in the market for Imperial Yellow, sir?" The Chinese clerk looked first at Hayden, then settled his question upon me. He was not your Charlie Chan younger son, but a tall, lithe, well-dressed young opportunist. He wore the same sleek, designer glasses as David Roth.

"No. I'm writing a book with an Imperial Yellow bowl as the centerpiece. I wanted to see one, perhaps touch one."

"They are very expensive."

There was no tag or card anywhere around the bowl, so I asked the price.

"Three hundred thousand."

"My grandmother had a similar bowl slightly larger than this one. She washed the lettuce and radishes in it until a friend told her of its worth."

"And you have it now?" His eyes glistened.

"No. She sold it forty years ago. To a shop in the Chinatown over by Union Station. I don't remember the name, an old father and his son."

"Many of my family were there. Perhaps an uncle or a cousin bought it."

Hayden paced around the store as I talked to the clerk. The information about my grandmother softened the clerk's initial resolve to keep me from touching the bowl, so he unlocked the plexiglass cube with a key on a chain. He lifted the cover gingerly and placed it down on a nearby counter.

The bowl glowed in the light from overhead, now not filtered by the cover. This was an object that collectors sought the world over, hoping to find the ill-informed shopkeeper on a back street. I knew that these bowls were all stolen, booty from the sack of imperial palaces by western troops. The emperor had never given up a single one of his yellow beauties on his own, all his treasures wrested away by foreign mercenaries, sent back to seafaring families in England or Nantucket.

The clerk brought a felt-covered board out onto the counter and carried the bowl with studied steps over onto it. Please be careful and do not lift it, he said.

I ran my finger along the lip of the bowl, exactly as I had seen the old merchant do when my grandmother presented her bowl to him for purchase. He went slowly around the circumference, presumably testing for chips or dents. Hayden had finished his tour of the store and came to watch. The whole circle was perfect. I asked the clerk to let me see the bottom the bowl, which he lifted and turned over. The yellow glaze changed to white, with blue Chinese characters.

The clerk said with authority, "It is Ming dynasty, about 1730." I continued looking, lightly touching it while the clerk watched my hand intently. Raising his eyebrows in a question if I was finished, he restored the bowl to its plinth, locked the cover. He gave me a printed provenance sheet with several photos, one which included a view of the bottom of the bowl.

Blue Chinese characters in two lines said that it was Ming Dynasty, early 18th Century.

The bowl had been in a ducal collection in an English country house until a year ago, the sheet said, the family de-accessioning with regret for funds to repair the extensive leaks to the lead roof. (Chinese gold turning into English lead, something wrong here). Nothing was mentioned of its meandering travels from Peking to a half-timbered mansion in Cornwall.

The last shop on Mountolive also had a yellow bowl, featured in the front display window. It was smaller than its sister in the other shop and a slightly different shade of yellow. It was clearly priced with a tent card in graceful cursive script, A Fine 18th C. Imperial Yellow Bowl, only 200K. If the shops did not actually collude on pricing, they all went to the same source.

"I think I have what I need without going in," I told Hayden. We walked back to the car and drove over to Benedict Canyon Road, following David's instructions. Press the button at the gates twice, he said, and they will open. Drive up the hill and you'll eventually see the house. He was standing by the door.

"What a spread, David. This is Hayden Danning. David Roth."

They shook hands and David said, "I bought it from an estate. It was built by a rich old Broadway dancer who had inherited a fortune from his even older lover, a Pittsburgh ball-bearing heir. His new, young Mexican lover had a good eye and designed all these walls and pavilions. The guest-house is right over there."

It was a faux Mayan temple with massive buttresses on each corner, a pair of entry doors that Maria Montez might have used in *Cobra Woman*, looking poignantly over her shoulder as she went, fetchingly dressed, to her horrible fate inside. The heavily-planted tropical garden crushed in around the house, large leaves flat against the windows.

Inside, the house was furnished in heavy pieces from the studio auctions, including a ten foot gilded Egyptian statue of a striding pharaoh, its base serving as a night table between the twin beds. A telephone and a stack of magazines nestled between his feet, goose-necked reading lights were affixed to each leg with an anklet. Zebra-print cotton spreads covered each bed, and a massive crystal chandelier, probably from a Jeanette McDonald musical, hung low enough to hit your head upon in the night.

David said, "I bought it completely furnished." This excused, I suppose, this mélange of warring elements. Hayden was delighted, the rumors of opulence and excess in the Babylon to the south were true. He said when David went back to the main house, "Wow. Ambrose has shown me pictures of places like this that some of his friends own." If Hayden did not know in so many words that his uncle was gay, he knew it intuitively.

Even the lap pool was done up as something else, the rounded ends coming high as the prow and stern of a marble ship. A Greek one, I supposed. David sat reading scripts under a nearby umbrella embroidered in a Greek key design, while we went for a swim. I got out after a few laps, Hayden staying the course for fifty more.

"When did you buy this house, David?" I dried off and joined him under the umbrella.

"Three years ago. I needed a place to entertain, let people know that KableOne was on the map. Appearance is everything in this business. The channel is paying for a cocktail party here tonight, you and Hayden are invited."

"So you are the CEO and principal investor? I'm impressed."

"Mattox, I had a natural touch for movie producing, and I was lucky."

"Luck is overrated, I think. I'll give you the credit."

He looked over at Hayden plowing through the water. "Is he your boy-friend?"

"No, I rent from him. Good-looking for a landlord, don't you think?"

"I could probably find a place for him somewhere, if you want."

"I think its better he just stays in Glitter Bay. Thanks, though." The thought passed through my mind that David was gay, but too many pieces did not fit. He may just have been asexual, a dedicated observer of the cinematic rituals. It would be a valuable asset for a producer to see clearly with dispassion and humor.

At the party, which started at ten o'clock, I had an early notion that Hayden was ill at ease. He stood away from the crowd in a corner of the small kitchen, self-conscious when people came up to converse. I hated to see his handsome face change to that of an unappealing child.

There were no first rank stars at David's gathering, only production people, the four young scriptwriters, and dozens of unknowns eager for high-level contacts, looking over shoulders as they talked. At first I walked among them, introducing myself and talking to whomever would respond, but I kept seeing Hayden out of the corner of my eye, alone. He looked miserable. I spent the rest of the evening, an hour or so, at his side and he was clearly relieved to have me there. A few of the other guests came up to us, but departed when it was clear that we were of no importance. Even Hayden's good looks were not enough to make a mark.

I told him, "We can do the Indian rope trick."

"What?"

"Disappear from the party, up the rope and away. Right through that door."

"Okay."

We edged out onto the terrace and retreated down the hill to the guest house. It was about midnight, and the music from the house above echoed through the foliage.

The guest house smelled stuffy in the night air, as if it needed a thorough cleaning out after years of once-over dustings. Hayden sat on the side of his bed and said, "Big parties make me nervous."

"Me, too."

"But you can talk to new people. I watched you introduce yourself to that group sitting by the lion fountain."

"They weren't very interesting."

"I could never do that. Walk up and say my name."

"When I was your age, an older friend told me that you never needed to worry in large parties of unknown faces. If you just stood, looking like you didn't care, a new friend would come over and introduce himself."

"But that didn't happen this time."

"Maybe we didn't wait long enough or didn't look properly unconcerned. The friend said that if nobody came up, it was their loss. We didn't miss anything, I am sure." I kissed him on the forehead, still furrowed.

Hayden closed his eyes and appeared to sleep under his striped spread, his social worries not of a grand enough scale to keep him awake. The pharaoh loomed up between us, and I could not give up a chance to read for a while under his ankle light. Proust seemed absolutely correct in this setting and I finished thirty pages before turning off the light. In the dark, Hayden came over to my bed. He gave me his body, turning his back to me under the zebra cover, almost a tribal submission under pharoah's gaze.

In the morning, after another long swim in the marble trireme, we decided to go right back to Glitter Bay early. Hayden stayed to finish his laps and I found David up at the main house. He was having toast and coffee on the east terrace. "We're heading back now, David. What a great party."

"Your friend did not have a good time."

"Glitter Bay is a small town, like Santa Fe. We aren't used to meeting such luminaries, to step on the velvet ladder."

"Bull shit, but I'm glad you came. I've been thinking, remembering. You did save me a lot in those early years; I was such a nerd. And I can see the humor."

"What humor?"

"You, the gay guy that everyone thought was straight, fighting battles for a straight guy, who everybody thought was gay."

"What do you make of that?"

"It's funny, that's all."

"I don't think anybody thinks you're gay now."

"But everybody still thinks you're straight. They all asked about you."

"Curious."

If David had emerged whole, repaired, from a sorrowful childhood, it was with a sharper eye than when he was a boy, an ability to see past the opaque facades that people in Hollywood erect, hoping to hide their flaws. He also saw the comedy in the human condition as it presented itself in the film world. Maybe that was a large part of his achievement in a business where the surface meant everything. I felt a kinship with David, both of us having survived a youth fraught with potholes and barriers. I did not consider myself a runaway success like David, however, only a survivor.

On the way back to Glitter Bay, we stopped for lunch at the old Santa Barbara hotel on the beach, replete with red-tiled roofs and manicured gardens. The dining room opened right onto the sea, perfect beach chairs in perfect rows, even the surf more obedient than elsewhere.

Hayden said, "You fit into so many worlds, Mattox. Laguna, Pasadena, Burbank, that expensive antique shop, Benedict Canyon, that party with all those people, here in Santa Barbara. I admire that."

"You fit in at Glitter Bay. You wear it like a well-tailored suit."

"I know, but I feel so clumsy everywhere else."

"I don't think you're clumsy."

"Everybody else does."

"You have a natural grace, Hayden. Like a stag walking through a thick forest, never faltering. The natural man in a natural world. It's okay that you feel dispossessed in the highly dysfunctional Benedict Canyon."

"It doesn't seem okay to me."

I put my hand on his arm. "In your heart, you want to please. Me, Ambrose, Garnet and even Sylvan. How can that be a bad quality? How is that ever clumsy?" I saw that earnest worry still in his eyes, the same that I saw so many times in Richard's. He feared that he was not adequate, not talented, that fortune would not smile.

How had David traveled so ably beyond his boyhood, and not these two men that I loved? Was it their wounded quality, vulnerability, that made me love them? Was I still playing doctor, eager for new wounded patients, to rub ointments on their damaged parts?

Wilfred told me once that I had a head-nurse syndrome. Anybody who was defenseless, at risk, could get right into my heart on a fast express. He said it was not a failing, exactly, but an odd characteristic. I think he really saw it as a failing.

It was true that I could never resist a handsome, burly man with worried eyes. Hayden was the small child that asked for help, so how could I leave him high and dry? If for only the rest of the summer, my role was clear.

22

Tuxedo World

The days to finish the book were diminishing, only weeks before the first of September and the end of my summer lease with Olivia. I had the second draft completed, printed the pages out and found a shop in Morro Bay that could bind them with black tape. It was easier for me do the final edit on a tape-bound manuscript, perhaps one psychological step closer to the actual printed book than loose pages, which could fly about in the drafty cottage if not weighted down. A bound manuscript was more portable as well, simple to read and annotate on the deck chairs in front of the cottage.

Laura had written on the white page across from the first draft's closing chapter:

The story skips over so much that I don't understand,
the why and what of the character's choices and actions.
There is not an interior thought process
that is shared with the reader.

Perhaps I now shared too much with the reader, letting the mind of the narrator open like the side of a breadbox, jumbled slices and unfinished loaves there for all to see. Untidy thoughts were of great interest to me, however, because they are the stuff of worry and grief, love and loss, the parts of life that resonate.

I had enlarged the book by a hundred pages, the opposite of the timeworn advice that the second draft must equal the first draft minus ten percent. The bound manuscripts, fresh from the copy shop, sat at the end of my writing table: fat, unsoiled, ready for comments and changes.

It was late in the morning, Hayden long away at work. I took the manuscript outside and sat in a deck-chair, cool in a patch of shade from the house, a cup of coffee on the adjoining table. The first thirty pages of editing went well, with only a few typographical errors, and a misuse of the word 'lay.' My friend Tukey would catch that if it survived my editing. The pace of the story pleased me, quickly taking up a good speed and continuing with a breeze and energy.

I had not heard his arrival in the parking spaces, but looked up from my pages to see Ambrose standing in front of me. "Mattox, may I bother you? I'm leaving for Greece tomorrow and won't have another time to talk."

"Please, Ambrose." He sat in the other deck chair.

"Is your book done?"

"Almost. I'm scribbling away at changes here and there. But it seems to lie well on the land."

"I expect you're thinking of leaving us, going back to Santa Fe."

"I am. Thoughts of home bubble up. I must start back soon. It's hard, because it's so damnably pleasant here, the zenith of a California summer."

"Maybe you'll stay on, then? Into September? October?"

"No, Ambrose. I learned a lesson early on that it's better to leave in the middle of the party, not after the last dog."

"It's Hayden I want to talk about. You and Hayden."

Would this be a diatribe on how naughty we were, how I had led a beloved nephew astray? How we had despoiled the bed night after night? I thought not. Why, then, did he want me to stay on into September?

He continued, "I think you have seen Hayden for what he is, a lost boy almost grown up. I know he can't give you what you need, a responsive lover, a sensual mate who can excite you and fulfill you. Few of us are lucky enough for that. But I have watched Hayden open up, blossom if you will, after you came here. It can't be a coincidence."

"I've grown to love Hayden."

140

"I believe that he returns your love, and is growing up because of you. Your presence gives him confidence. I know it, and Sylvan knows it. She has come to fear a change in her brother's affections, and sees his love for you as a threat."

"I have sensed that from her this last week."

"She had her chance at love, partnership, but gave it up. I won't let her ruin Hayden's chance. If you stayed on a bit longer, Hayden would understand what it is to love, to love you. A high plateau of happiness, if only for a while. I never had it, but I want it for Hayden."

"You put it very well. I wish I could offer that to Hayden. I can't."

"How about making a place for Hayden in your life? Don't just drive away from here like everybody else. Could you ask him to go to Santa Fe with you, at least for a while? Part-time with Mattox will be better than none at all."

Ambrose was being the compleat uncle (or was it Dolly Levi), arranging for happiness and love, pushing a connection further than it chose to go on its own. I did want to have Hayden with me, to feel his love protecting me, but there were so many problems involved that I could not even begin to list them. I would not let myself imagine that we could live together just because we shared a physical lust and some comfortable dinner talk. And there was the not so small matter of Hayden's being basically straight, only slightly bent.

Maybe Richard was my only time for love, and another could not grow on the same spot. Roses were said to wither and die in the same planting space as a bush that had died there before. I should settle for my work, let it be my lover from now on.

I said, "Ambrose, I will try. I want that to happen, believe me, but right now I see a path littered with difficulties. Let me think about it." Wilfred said that whenever I said "let me think about it," I really meant "no." But I didn't mean "no" this time.

"Thanks, Mattox. Call me in Mykonos with what you decide. I've written down the number of the Hotel Poseidon, it's eight hours later than here. Whatever it is, I'll respect your decision."

I walked with him to his car. He said he had waited longer than usual for his summer away, needed a bit of brightness. I thought that was a lovely euphemism for drinking everything in sight, dancing till dawn every night, getting bedded with regularity. Here's to brightness, I said as he drove away, waving.

It was strange that he could not help his nephew more. Hayden was not gay, but he could learn a lot from a savvy mentor about love. I guess that Ambrose was not really savvy, not really a mentor. He had problems with his own life, unresolved emotional issues that overwhelmed his ability to comfort others.

It was hard to get back into the flow of my book again, real life dulling the edge on my fiction. I spent the rest of the day getting my papers in order, organizing the books I had brought with me, looking up words that I was sure that I had misused in *Imperial Yellow*, running the SpellChek/GrammarChek program through the whole manuscript again. Yes, I did want to spell a name that way, every time, irregular as it was, and no, I did not want to change out of the passive voice. Are you sure? Be that as it may.

It was still afternoon, when I heard Hayden's car in the driveway, an early arrival home. At the door, he said, "Let's go have a drink at the Kamikaze. I'll buy you dinner."

"No, it's my turn." He was insistent, however.

It was Happy Hour as we sat at the bar with Sylvan. After she served us, working orders for the other patrons at top speed, she often glanced our way. Finally, she took a break and brought her stool down to our end, a diet Coke on ice.

Hayden said, "Crazy night, huh?"

"What are you guys up to?"

"Dinner at the café. Want to join us?"

"The bar won't clear out in time. Come back here for a night-cap. I want to talk to you both."

"Why not now?"

"No, later. It's too noisy, too distracted."

We finished our drinks and drove to the café for dinner. I felt Hayden looking at me a lot without saying anything, as if he expected something extraordinary to come out of the top of my head. In the same manner, Richard would ask me what I was thinking about. I could never answer with truth, the disorganized rush of thoughts so different from talk. How could I pick among the dozens of topics that bumped up against each other in my mind, interfolding and reacting, to say that this is the one I was thinking about? Nothing important, Richard.

After dinner, we went back to the Kamikaze. Sylvan walked over to join us at the table, brought us each another drink. Hayden had been thinking about my departure, I was sure. He was a proud person, and would not bring it up in hopes of dissuading me.

Instead, he said, "I was thinking about a summer when Sylvan and I were small, after dad died. Ambrose took us fishing in the marshlands whenever he could. Remember that, Syl?" He put his hand over on hers.

She nodded.

He continued, "We kept seeing a large water-bird, taller than a gray heron, very strange for these parts. He was black and white, formal and court-like. We called him the Duke of Wellington, because that was the only titled name we knew."

She said, "The whole village talked about him. Ambrose thought he might a whooping crane, miles off his migration. We watched him every day through the binoculars. He was stand-offish from the start, though, stayed away from us, on the other side of the marsh."

Hayden said, "He sensed that he did not belong here, but he also saw that the backwaters were full of fish, and that made him happy. Ambrose said that he was an elegant, poised bird, not like the sand-hill cranes we were used to."

I knew where this was heading and wanted to interrupt. Hayden put a hand over on my arm to stop me.

He continued, "After a couple of months of feeding and preening for us locals, one day Wellington abandoned us. Nobody saw him leave. He just disappeared into his black and white, tuxedo world. Just like you."

Here was Hayden at his lyrical best, in his spare way getting right to the point, right into the heart. Even Sylvan seemed quiet, not attacking, as had maybe been her plan.

He said, "What do you think of that, Mattox? Is he just like you? Are you going to leave us?"

I had nothing to say in my defense. Richard had abandoned me, and now I was doing the same thing to Hayden. Tears did not actually appear, but a prelude to them glazed my eyes. Seeing my distress, he was immediately sorry he had brought up such a reaction, put his hand on my shoulder.

I asked, "Did he ever come back? The next summer?"

"No. Not until now."

"Don't over-do it, Hayden. Yes, I feel awful about leaving."

"Then don't. Stay on with me, Sylvan will get used to us being together."

She did not look up, "I do like you better than any of Hayden's girl-friends, Mattox. I almost said 'other' girl-friends. I couldn't help being jealous, feeling left out, though. Something close was building up, a barrier between Hayden and me. I saw it happening slowly and knew that I was not part of it."

I said, "I have to go back to Santa Fe, but, unlike Wellington, I will be back."

Hayden said, "Promise?"

"I do promise."

"I wish I could be gay, be your lover, but that's not really me. I still want you to know that I need your love."

I knew that I was more like Wellington than I could admit, spending the summer feeding on the fingerlings at Glitter Bay, but never intending to stay. A summer idyll, a brief encounter; Noel Coward could be laughing at us, brittle amusement from his banquette in the sky. Would I really be back as I promised?

144

Sylvan appeared to accept the situation, stop her anger. I wondered how much the surety of my departure had to do with it? She hugged me when we left the bar. Hayden asked her what it was she wanted to tell us, but she said nothing important. What part of our discussion covered what she wanted to say?

In the car on the way back to the beach, Hayden said. "I really enjoy our time in bed together. At first I did it hoping to trap you, to make you love me. I was serious when I told you and Syl that I wish I could turn gay and be your lover. To keep you loving me."

"Ambrose came by today, wanted me to stay on with you too. If I couldn't, he asked me to make a place in my life for you. "

"Good for him. What did you say?"

"That there already is a place for you. Here on Glitter Bay."

Hayden wants me to stay on as a companion, not a gay one because he really is not that way. He cannot change, much as he would like. So I will become the happy groupie, adoring this sensual resource for the whole community, waiting patiently for my turn. Is that what a harem was? Unhappy attendees around the village well, hiding their expressions behind folds of cloth? Much as I want you, Hayden, no thanks.

After parking the car, we walked through the banana grove, a slight breeze rustling the leaves. Richard always thought that the sound of banana leaves in Barbados was ominous, night-borne, full of evil portent, but I never heard what he was talking about. Men with knives, he said, waiting in the moving leaves. Bridget did not like the sound of rustling leaves either, as I recall.

23

Old Pecking Order

It was late morning on the next day, a covered day with thin, high clouds. I thought about a last swim in my perfect pool two coves to the south, found a towel and started the walk down the beach. The century plant beside the vegetable garden was in full bloom, the ivory white blossoms opening in the night. Morris would be excited.

As I walked farther, Garnet was out on her terrace, all of her French doors propped open. I waved and pointed to the south, where the pool awaited. She nodded, understanding my destination, and I continued on to the second cove, the water still cold and clear, but not as blue under the cloudy sky.

This time no thoughts from the past burrowed up from the bottom of my mind as before; future plans about being back in Santa Fe crowding them out. I knew that having a boyhood in California did not guarantee that I would return, even in time I would not find a place here in the middle of my memories. Remembrance had lost its hold.

I dried off with the towel and walked back to Garnet's cottage. I said good morning and sat in the chair beside her.

She said, "You have a finality in your step. Something in your body language."

"I put a finish on the second draft a few days ago, so I'm thinking thoughts of home. I'll be leaving soon."

"I was wrong. It's you who walks away from the love machine, not the other way around."

"Hayden and I have been talking about how to keep our friendship alive, from afar."

"It won't stay alive. Not the same way."

"I know."

"It was a classic summer-at-the-beach movie, the handsome life-guard bedding the new girl, making her cry when she has to go back to the big house with foundation plantings in the suburbs, iron fences, gates across the driveway. She goes on with her life and friends, but always with thoughts of the life-guard's tanned body in the shaded life boat, a tryst away from the others."

It was better to leave it there. I recognized her scenario, with Sandra Dee and Tab Hunter, and we both smiled. Garnet would not be unhappy to see me go, generous as she had been in sharing Hayden with me. She liked the old pecking order on the beach, her at the top, Hayden second and the other cottagers in descending order below. An orderly scene out of English court life, everything cascading down from the queen, sitting on high with her riches and her favorite at her side. Bette Davis at her best.

She said, "Sylvan will be in high spirits. She can regain her dear Hayden. But your visit here has been good for us, it's rattled all our cages."

"I don't think that I was ever a threat. Although Glitter Bay is your universe, you allow Hayden to be its hub. Around him all the planets circle."

"Don't get too syrupy, Mattox."

"Okay. I'll miss you the most, after Hayden."

"Maybe you should rent one of my cottages, when one comes vacant. Just to keep a toe-hold on Glitter Bay. We need a chronicler of events, our Hedda Hopper. The beach life agrees with you and you must admit you got some work done."

"I would like that. Will you put my name on the list?"

"It's done."

I thought that it was the last time I would see Garnet. The notion occurred to me that everyone I had met on Glitter Bay was afraid of me, anxious that I would upset the status quo of their little world. Sylvan certainly was, Garnet in a more pleasant way, on the surface accepting me and my involvement with Hayden, but down deep wanting me to go away, to have what went before restored.

Henry Clarence had offered his low-key welcome and Morris was too young to care. Ambrose was uneasy that I would expose him and what he did on those faraway nights of Mykonos. Hayden himself, although fascinated with what he saw of my world, what he imagined me to be, was fearful of a life that included me.

I kissed Garnet and walked back to Hayden's end of the beach. Morris and Henry were already at it on a ladder, measuring the flower on its high stem, the circumference of the stalk and the full height of the inflorescence. The flower stood taller than the top of Hayden's roof, a buzz from the insects circling it. Morris wrote the details in her notebook, now soiled and dog-eared from a summer of pseudo-science.

What an earnest young girl she was; I wondered if science would continue to interest her or would a handsome California boy catch her eye, a charmer like Hayden who would bring joy and unhappiness in equal measure.

I asked her, "When do you give your report?"

"Next week. School starts on Monday."

"So soon? I remember September school days when I went to school."

"They say we must have more time in school now."

Henry winked at me. "They're smarter, you know. We were just the Dumbo generation who couldn't fight a war or run a nation. We're all anxious to turn things over to the new little geniuses, let them do things better."

I said, sensing his irony. "Wouldn't that be nice, to turn over the world?"

"Garnet says you're leaving soon."

"Soon, Henry."

"I still think you have a place here, in Hayden's house."

"I wish it would work."

Morris said, "Garnet thinks you'll be back. She said so."

"Who's to question Garnet?"

Maybe a woman with the prescience to buy up a whole California beach at fire-sale prices should be listened to. The approval process along the beach was complete. I should just relent and become another bride in Hayden's Harem. I could not wait to see the expression on Wilfred's face when I told him. I've decided, my dear, to give up my Santa Fe house and move in with Mr. Fixit, who repairs things every night. I'll give away my paintings and the easel and learn to make tortillas and put hems on dish-towels.

My summer report was also finished. I had topped out just like the century plant. Did wrapping up on one front mean that there was the same going on all fronts?

I said to them, "I'll see you again before I go. Keep up with the measuring."

Back at my writing table, the energy had departed from the neat stacks of books, papers and folders. The project was done. I should call New York, see what Laura knew of the business in Burbank.

"Mattox. I'm glad you called."

"I'll be leaving Glitter Bay and going back to Santa Fe."

"There's news about KableOne."

"What?"

"David Roth has been promoted, will work here in New York, right under the chairman. He's been in the city for a week."

"Sounds ominous, doesn't it, 'right under the chairman?' I see an unhappy minion in blue pajamas in the Cultural Revolution."

"Not bad news for you, actually. Brenda has taken over as CEO in Burbank. She's fast-tracking your stories for production in Santa Fe next month, and they have taken out one of the stories, the one about Cecily Brompton."

"Why?"

"She's chosen to make a separate TV movie of that, so is reserving it for next year. This is the new CEO making her mark, drawing some lines in the sand. I've been negotiating a separate payment for that. You will be pleased, I am sure."

"So much happens when I hide away at the beach. I should keep doing it."

"I'll let you know how it goes with Brenda."

"I like her."

"She likes you, too."

I wondered how many strong-woman stories would be opted by the new KableOne, a new direction under a new captain.

24

No Umbrellas

I woke early, the sky still washed with black, Hayden asleep beside me. We had now spent many nights sleeping together, Hayden offering himself as a sensual gift that I explored with gratitude. He was completely devoid of attitude about it, a gift that gave pleasure, had worth for its recipient. He never snored, exactly, but made intermittent breathing sounds when he slept. It was now a week before the end of August, my second draft was finished, three hundred seventy-six pages, two copies printed out and bound in black tape. If my life pattern was to leave on the perihelion, I ought to go this morning. Everything after this would be repetitious, downhill from here, the sun dimming each day, less joy with each sunrise.

Watching Hayden beside me, I recounted the things I needed to pack. It could be done in half an hour. Was it me or someone else who proclaimed, as a callow student, full of himself, that in life we should own only the chattel that would fit in the back of a car, preferably a VW or a Morris Minor? Everything else was vanity, frippery, weight around the ankles. How could a person loft, attain the heights, with heavy suitcases in each hand?

I would drive down the coast to Laguna to be with Dominic for a night or two, to experience the rest that California was offering me, before going over the hills to Palm Springs. Should I feel guilty leaving Hayden for Dominic? Curiously, I did not. It would be a long day, but entirely possible if I got an early start.

A pearlescent shading came into the western sky, matching the glow of the rising sun behind us. Hayden had awakened and was looking at me. He said, "You're leaving today, aren't you?

"Yes. It's time."

"You're a hard man to trap, Mattox. You just squirrel your way out. You, and your Indian Rope Trick."

"Thank you for my last night."

"True lovers shouldn't have to thank each other." He and Richard coming up with the same lines again. A passing thought winged through my mind, that these two men were but one person, I had experienced only one half at a time. Was that possible? One dark-haired, the other light, a yin and yang that passed through my life, one after the other. Perhaps mocking me.

I said, "I've printed out a copy of my book for Ambrose. It's on the work table."

"I'll see he gets it when he gets back. May I read it, too?"

"Of course. I should say it's your copy. Ambrose can borrow it."

"You're actually going?"

"In about an hour."

He said, "What a great summer. Mattox. It would not have happened if you hadn't come into Sylvan's bar, stayed down in Santa Barbara or Laguna instead."

"For me, too."

"I liked you the first day we met. Who would have thought how much?"

"Maybe you can visit me in Santa Fe."

"I don't think so. You can come back here. I like you in my place and don't know what it would be like in yours."

"That's right. I'll come back here."

He kissed me, not our first, but one of our few. Hayden had that built-in fear that all straight men have who experiment with the gay life: they can do anything else, assume all positions, partake all activities, think all thoughts, use any lotion but kissing meant they had gone queer. If you kiss you cannot go back. No kissing, just like the rule for officers in the Air Force, no umbrellas. Some general in the Joint Chiefs knew that umbrellas were the sure sign of the fag. Had he vacationed on Mykonos, too, away from the Pentagon?

He said, "Let me ask you something."

That was a preamble I had learned to dread. It usually meant that the inquisitor was reticent or ashamed to ask, first looking for permission to proceed. "What, Hayden?"

"Do you think Ambrose is gay?"

How does he not know, after living with me for a summer, seeing how a homosexual thinks? Of course, Ambrose was gay. It was not up to me to out him, however.

"Do you think he is?"

"Yes. He doesn't want me to know, though."

"He leads a closeted life ⁄ college professor, mentor to the young. He travels half⁄way around the world to be himself, and he believes that it might be unwise, for whatever reasons, for him to come out at his age. He's called a closet queen."

"But being gay doesn't bother you. You're out, to everybody you meet. I've heard you say it several times, I'm gay."

"I believe in that. I've purposely chosen in life to do the work that doesn't require you to lie about it, to act straight just to keep your job. Nobody cares what painters and writers do. Teachers may have to lie, because sometimes small colleges are not so tolerant, boards of directors with mean thoughts. I've been lucky."

"I don't imagine it is luck with you."

"No, it really isn't. I thought about it, made that decision, early in my life."

"Should I ask Ambrose about it, tell him that I know?"

"Absolutely. Truth is always better, especially with the ones you love."

"Then, what about you and me, our sex together? Should I tell him about that, too?"

"If he brings it up, I wouldn't deny it. I think he already knows."

"I wish you would stay. I know now what having a center means. I was always circling around a void before, nothing there. But with you, I feel a strength in the hub. My heart lifted when I came in the door night after night, that Mattox is here. The Mattox that loves me is still in my house. We'll have a night together."

His ability to get right into the middle of a song was still there. "I felt it too."

"There's no way you can stay on, is there?" He had those pleading eyes again, those guileless, expectant eyes that opened up right down to the soul. I knew it hurt his ever-present pride to show me this.

"No, Hayden. But we will stay together, I'll call every day as soon as I get home."

"It won't be the same. Your stillness won't be in my house."

"Let's see how it goes."

"I know already."

25

A Skittish Deer

Although Hayden could drive to Laguna in four hours, with his expert weaving in and out of the freeway melee, it took me six hours on my own. Already I was missing what he had to offer. It was late afternoon when I arrived. Midweek, there were plenty of parking places near Dominic's restaurant. I found one and walked over to the open door of the bar.

A small group of women murmured together in the near stools, the afternoon smell of bars redolent, and the dining rooms were dark, the restaurant in rest mode, a sleeping lion. I looked around for Dominic or the older woman with the hair-do who manned the gates to the dining rooms. Nobody. I looked into the kitchen and the staff there did not speak enough English for my questions. They nodded when I asked for Dominic. Si, si, Dominic.

Perhaps the bar-tender was the man to ask. I sat on the same stool as before; he was fully engrossed telling a story to the three women, gesticulating for a fish story, hands apart about two feet, or was it another subject? He saw me, and after he cashed in the punch line to his tale, came over to my end of the bar while he looked back at the women laughing and clapping.

I asked him, "When does Dominic come in?"

"Not tonight. He's in Cabo San Lucas until tomorrow."

"Ouch. I should have called."

"He was expecting you?"

"I was here in July, told him I would be back in late August. Nothing definite."

"He and Stewart went down there for a break before Labor Day. What can I get you to drink?"

"Nothing, thanks. Who's Stewart?"

"Dominic's partner."

"Oh."

"You wouldn't have met him in June or July. He was in Scotland until October. His family has a big house there, at least that's what he says. Dominic's been running the place on his own, a real bummer."

"So he and Stewart have this business together. I didn't know."

"Stewart came back early, just to help out. They're good guys to work for. No problems. Best wages in Laguna, even a dental plan." He smiled big to show his perfect teeth.

"I'll bet. Maybe I'll have a beer after all. Budweiser."

"You got it."

While I poured the beer into the frosted class, foam slowly subsiding, I contemplated my loss of innocence. The sad-eyed Dominic, a brother in grief, was just looking for a quick piece of ass before Stewart came home. So much for cozy trips back to Cyprus to meet the folks, to help with the olive harvest. Who usually stayed in the converted studio, the plein air painter's cottage that was perfect for me? Was it the newest trick?

Love was a canny one to follow, like a skittish deer running this way and that, luring you deeper into his woods, promising you hidden pools of warm delight, overhanging willows, then jumping high over the underbrush to disappear entirely. He had successfully eluded me once again. Or was it his brother, Lust, that I had been following? They both were slippery, able to lure then disappear.

I asked the bartender for a California map; I remembered that there was a minor highway that zig-zagged across to the Coachella Valley, but I could not recall the city it departed from. There it was, Highway 74, from San Juan Capistrano, just south of Laguna, through thick and thin to Palm Desert, about 100 miles. There should be three hours of light left.

"Thanks," I called down to the bartender, "tell Dominic and Stewart that I came by. So sorry to miss them. Name's Mattox." He wrote it down on a note-pad beside the computer and gave me a thumb's up sign. I left him a ten dollar tip to make sure the message got through. Let Dominic explain that to Stewart.

Highway 74 was a mess from the start, poorly marked and apt to disappear in unmarked suburbs for blocks, emerging in unexpected turnings. It went right through small towns, orange and avocado groves, red-roofed housing developments, old market towns with Sears Roebucks stores, and without warning, a long stretch of unspoiled wooded canyons with running streams under sycamore trees.

I decided not to call Bob Dermott, who disliked anything sudden in his life, but would book into one of the motels along Palm Canyon Drive. There was a large establishment with a California mission theme and a vacancy sign, the office like a small chapel, arched windows and a running fountain next to the entry door. The sun had set, and, when I stepped out of the air-conditioned car, I was hit with a wall of dry heat. A bank sign down the way flashed the temperature. 110F. 31C. 110F. 31C.

The room was hot and airless, but the desk clerk explained how to start the AC. It would be cool in five minutes. I was tired from the miles and emotion of the day and I knew better than to take a quick nap. I would look for an open restaurant and have an early meal, earlier than most Palm Springers, who hunkered down in their cool houses until ten on summer nights. Like Madrid or Tangiers.

I drove past Davy's Locker where Bob and I had dinner several months ago, but it was dark. The Italian restaurant nearby was closed, as well as the Bombay Express, the Mogul-sized front door locked up with a steel mesh over-door. I spotted a Mexican restaurant in the middle of town with water-misters high across the front terrace, the seated diners barely visible in the fog. I had an enchilada plate with an icy-cold Dos Equis beer, savoring the intermittent drifts of moist coolness across my table, not exactly the same as coastal fog.

As I neared sleep in the cold motel room, it occurred to me that

California was throwing me out, unhappy with the native son who found lacking so many of its amenable features. You no like our handsome men, faithless handsome men, that is, expensive freeways, cold sea-waters and hot, hot desert, then you not welcome. Sleep was winning, and I knew that in the morning I would run, early and full-speed, back to Santa Fe, a long day of driving, a horse back to his barn.

I could see Axton's face across from me in the booth at Davy's, smiling widely with his big hands over on mine; I heard his bass voice again with an aria of persuasion, join the brotherhood of sensuality, Mattox, make love for a night and forget. A faint murmur of desire stirred in my mid-section as I thought about him.

Nirvana, perhaps, for only a few days if I postponed the gallop back to my hay-lined stall. I could have hours of love with his perfect body, older but firm, more talented than his younger competitors. He could bring me forward, open previously unexplored levels of joy. Should I or shouldn't I? Even in exhaustion I was aroused, ready for Axton's ministrations. What secrets, what techniques had he learned that brought about that cocky assurance, what tricks of love? What exotic ports had taught him their secrets, this fly-boy with the big cock and vintage body? Where did I write down his telephone number? Tomorrow, I would decide tomorrow. The wish for love and sex had departed, exhausted with what was offered. Sleep.

26

A Third Grandmother

As I drove up La Bajada Hill fifteen miles south of Santa Fe, I knew it was said to be the steepest incline in New Mexico, only recently tamed by modern road-builders. I thought of the Depression migrants, on the northern, cooler way to the coast, who foundered on its steep switchbacks, gray Chevrolet four-cylinder sedans with seven hot passengers and steaming radiators. The long wait went on and on while the car cooled itself, all doors open, family stranded in this wasteland, precious drinking water wasted to dampen the billows of steam.

I felt the thankless wretch, spurning the California that they were trying so hard to reach. A spoiled, modern-day, good-for-nothing whose every whim must be met, lest he pout and become peevish. A man who had not found the exactly right love on the coast, this one too forward, this one too straight, this one too involved. A dust-storm would do you good, Mattox, pocking your windshield and making you cough. That thankless part of me stepped hard on the accelerator pedal and raced up the hill, past the ghosts fanning themselves beside the road.

From the top, I saw the low, sanguine sun turning the mountains the red-orange of the Lord's blood, or perhaps the pinkish-red of a sliced-open watermelon, confusing to the Spanish with which name to call them, the Sangre de Cristos or the Sandias. How glad I was to see the town nestled up against the mountains, still there. It was not a dream, a fable, not a small backwater that might disappear in an up-surge of song. Santa Fe existed, with its ancient, deep-rooted apple trees, ditches with gurgling mountain waters and eroding adobe walls. Home, my earthen-walled Ithaca of the high desert. Had I really been away just three months or was it twenty years?

It had rained earlier, pockets of water along the roadside reflecting the cadmium sky, and the damp smell of midsummer filled the car. Canyon Road was shiny with moisture, rivulets running down the sides, fallen leaves and twigs the evidence of a down-pour. Clouds crackled with lightning over the mountains, but the storm was moving on to the east, to bring others the same benediction.

The green sign pointed away from the road, *Mattox Williams Studio, 300 Feet.* Gravel crunched under my wheels, not that distinctive sharp crack of Hayden's oyster shell drive, but a softer, rounded, more feminine sound as I drove down the lane. River gravel: brown, tumbled, oval, and compliant.

Olivia Montelle's car was not in the parking space for the house, so she must be doing practice scales in the wings of the opera stage, orchestra tuning up the first act, or out for a dinner with smart companions, waiters drying the rainwater off the chairs. It was good that she was gone, because I did not want to talk about music, stagecraft or her perfect pitch right now. The drive from Palm Springs was easy for a younger man, but a twelve-hour trial for me.

The studio smelled of being closed for the summer, not hot, but locked and stuffy. I unlatched the back windows and the French doors, propped them open with the nearby bricks standing ready for just that purpose. Immediately a breeze filtered through the rooms, back to front, cool, sweeping out the disregard, disfavor of a summer closing. It blew up the items push-pinned onto my bulletin board, invitations to spring opening-night receptions (Meet the artist, a stunning new addition to Santa Fe Scene!), agendas of the Historic Review Board, lists of seeds to order (Italian Rosso lettuce, Bok Choy), photos of Mykonos (Richard and me on a morning-lit wall above Super Paradise Beach), Bali, red poppies (a long row of them from last year), and Black Mesa.

There were four rooms in the studio, the large painting space with a twelve-foot ceiling and an east-facing bank of casement windows, a small bedroom that I used for an office, the day-bed pushed against the wall, a bathroom with an old-fashioned London tub, so long and deep that I could float like a Madame Bonnard, naked and saturated with an opaline color, and a galley kitchen with a two-foot wide stove and a refrigerator that needed defrosting.

A kindly old woman who loved me like a son had built it, young then, for her own studio sixty years ago, and it remained the perfect place to make art, classic proportions for the doors and a noble ceiling of carved beams, with cherubim-headed corbels. She had learned her painting craft, taken courses in traditional wood-carving and absorbed the love of Greek revival matters at the Museum School in Philadelphia in the plummy years before 1929.

On a ladder, she carved with a simple chisel and hammer, *Ars longa, vita brevis,* along the side of a beam, then sculpted a perfect corner-bead along its entire length. I always felt that I had the Golden Rectangle on my side as I painted, a demi-god who smiled when I applied a telling stroke and frowned when my hand faltered.

The studio would be a place to wait out the few days remaining on Olivia's lease. I felt the need for a time of hidden nurture, quiet. I often had the day-dream about giving up the garden-encircled main house, the one that Olivia now occupied, simplifying upkeep and worry, and living solely in the close, graceful quarters of the studio. A simple bed like a monk's, thin soups from the narrow stove, Spartan happiness; instead, life keeps getting more complex rather than unadorned.

The easel in the studio held the white canvas, unpainted and waiting, that I had put there three months ago on departure day, a reminder to me of priorities. Painting first, writing next, then friends, then family, city, nation, world...or maybe friends should be just above writing, family at the bottom.

Richard told me that it was paramount to keep painting at the top of my list, that it was what defined everything else. I have not changed, Richard, you must not worry, the trip to California was a sojourn of no concern. Your Mattox was still the painter foremost, but he sometimes writes, sometimes makes love as well.

There was a bottle of white wine in the refrigerator. After testing, I poured out a large glass. It was somewhere along the road to vinegar, but still drinkable. The canvas seats of the director's chairs on the terrace outside of the studio were damp, but it felt good sitting down on my own terrace, listening to the night sounds.

The old building started to do its work, soothing me and offering me shelter. It cosseted me like a third grandmother: sit in me for a while, Mattox, absorb my ambience, my lavender scent; sleep against my white-plastered walls; wash in my claw-footed, porcelain-enclosed waters; ease your heart, my dear. Was that the function of these elaborate Greek cornices and multi-paned windows, to calm and welcome the returning grandson, feeling wounded as he tromped in, dirty and dusty from the Ionian Sea? I thought that it must have been.

The phone rang. It was Wilfred.

"I was worried with you on the road."

"I just a minute ago got in, still unpacked but with a glass of wine on the terrace."

"Good. I promise I won't keep you."

"Is everything all right?"

"Yes, but loads of gossip. Long stories with lurid details wait for you tomorrow. I talked with your Hayden in Glitter Bay, at last. A charmer, I must say. I got the word that you were on the road."

"How did you get his unlisted number?"

"Laura got it for me. She summoned it up like magic from Yahoo, using what little we knew. In the 'search for' window, she entered 'man, 35 years, banana-groves, power-plant employee, Glitter Bay, California,' and it came right up. I would have added 'blue-collar stud, not-so-very-straight, lays Mattox on regular basis,' but she was successful in her inexact way."

"How was he?"

"I could hear a wild party in the background, music, girls laughing, celebrating your departure, no doubt. That dreadful man who monopolized Hayden is finally gone."

"Can it, Wilfred. How was he?"

"He was fine, said that he was missing you. He has a great voice, by the way, all gravelly and in-your-face. I can see why you were so taken."

"I'm pooped now. We'll talk more in the morning."

"Glad you're back."

I shook out the sheets on the bed, perfect for house spiders, and banged the pillows together in a cloud of three-month dust. Mattox was taking back the ownership of his studio. I turned off all the lights before getting into bed, even the faintest glimmer might bring Olivia over, chatty from her night out, full of opera news. Sleep and home, at last. Hayden was still there, in my mind, but fading, smaller. Richard was still there, too, not fading very much for a dead person, but it did not hurt so much for him to be there.

27

Hithering Spill

I woke to the nearby sounds of a neighbor's house-building, hammers pounding, electric saws cutting through framing lumber and a jackhammer spasmodically bumping a section of concrete. For a town with four hundred years of history, Santa Fe kept a record number of new building projects going, small cottages that needed larger bathrooms, driveways that called out for two-car garages and walls that wanted pushing out for a gourmet kitchen. Owners were not settling for the awkward charm or dated mechanics of the small-roomed houses that honey-combed the East-side, expanding and up-dating them. New-comers wanted the authentic look of the streets near Canyon Road, but sought the gourmet kitchen and marble-lined master bath, too.

There was a can of coffee in the freezer, frost-encrusted, enough left to make a pot of dusty-tasting coffee. The cool mornings of late August had already started, tuning up for an early snow, I guessed. I thought about my late neighbor, Ignacio Montano, of whom I asked the same question every year, leaning over the fence while he picked the white peaches of late summer.

What does winter hold for us, Ignacio? Terrible, terrible winter. Deep snow, like it used to be, before you Anglos came. Get your firewood early, we will all run out. Despite his biblical predictions and imbedded hopes for a frozen doom, the winters were getting warmer and warmer, no deep freezes.

In the old Santa Fe mind of Ignacio, immoral acts during the summer months, cavortings in the orchards, straying hands on dark porches, were what brought on the severity of the following winter, the season of Vatican punishments, not the mere tilting and turning of the planets. Christian goodness might turn the odds in our favor, ever so slightly.

Olivia would not be up and around so early. Opera people were night people, sleeping with black-out masks, covering the east-facing windows with dark draperies. I would have several hours before having to confront her.

The pile of mail that Ramiro had collected stood two feet high, magazines, third-class fliers all messily intermingled with the few first-class letters. Why couldn't he learn to sort them out into neat piles? Maybe I was lucky to have anybody who would perform such a task at all.

I took my coffee into the studio room and sat looking at the easel, with its white canvas ready. I knew the muses of painting felt hurt at being ignored for three months, their sister in charge of writing getting all the attention. The painting girls would wreak their revenge, however, making my hand shaky, inaccurate as it got going again and turning the color mixtures to mud instead of the exquisite shades that were in my mind. I would have to pay penance to them, starting slowly like a beginner, throwing away the first attempts, finally breaking through when they thought I had been punished enough. He's been away from the easel again, sisters, searching for love and redemption, let's give him what-for.

I would start work now, a more important task than sorting the mail. The sooner I got the punishment phase over with the sooner my life would seem to be back on track. The book was done for now, a second draft, fat with an unsullied cover, that I would send without comment to Laura soon. Tomorrow, perhaps.

Life at home - it was a machine that had remained idle for a summer and would need oiling and encouragement to get going again. Richard was still there sitting in the studio chair, watching me paint, reading a book about the Clear Light of Bliss by a holy man who just made it out of Tibet to the safety of Dharamsala. It did not hurt anymore that he was there. He would be there, watching, commenting, the rest of my life, more than a shade and considerably less than a live companion.

I mixed the first color, raw sienna with cadmium red light, some green to pull it back, a perfect hue to draw the first lines. It was an effort to make the color just right. The tubes of paint fought me, required that I push a screw-driver down the dried end to the pliant paint beneath, each tube complaining in its own way about my summer away. Every movement had weights attached, heaviness that was not there when I had painted every day.

A landscape had been loitering my mind, asking to be brought into the light, a sunlight-raked mesa above, the iconic image of the west, with a complicated foreground to offset its jutting simplicity. A strong anthem at the top against a pizzicato fugue below. I would start with the bold shape of the mesa in bright light, demanding a dark shadow on the far side, replete with dark purples and maroons, and work down to the hithering spill at the bottom, rocks and broken sticks falling off the canvas towards me. The spill would bring the eye in, tease it to travel up.

From the house next door, Ben had heard my movements in the studio, vaguely remembering who I was, and he came in with many cries of unhappiness. Only a full ten minutes of attention would assuage him, the bonding he was accustomed to before our mutual summer of discontent. He was fatter, and perhaps noisier, but he had not switched his loyalties to opera. Sweetmeats and arias did not sit well, obviously.

Late in the afternoon there was a knock on the studio door. It was Olivia, who had seen my car parked in the studio space. She was clad in a bright terra-cotta kaftan, with long panels of cloth cascading from each shoulder. Her hair was a deep, chestnut-red now, but it was still in the theatrical, abundant curls. Did I see a Greek role coming up for her this fall, Clytemnestra or the Medea?

"Mattox, the opera house in Stuttgart caught fire last week and my contract there was cancelled. I have three weeks of down-time until the next engagement, and I could work more easily here than in New York. May I carry on here? I will pay you double rent, of course."

"Please stay. The studio is very comfortable for me."

"Fabulous. If you need any pots and pans, china or silver from the house, please come over and get them."

"The studio kitchen still has its cookery, plates and the like from the woman who built it sixty years ago. It all seemed to belong here, so I never changed things. I will manage fine, Olivia."

"Splendid. Ben must have found you, because he has been absent all morning."

"He did, with loud complaints about my leaving him for the summer."

"All my fish-balls and chicken treats for naught."

"Cats have no honor."

"I will call you about drinks one night soon. I feel that you're a brother now, my dear, because your house has given away all your secrets." Disloyal house to do that.

"I would like that." We kissed the ceremonial kiss of new acquaintance, a stagey cheek-to-cheek, and she was off.

28

Dickens on the Left

I had been back in Santa Fe for two weeks, painting every day from the early morning until noon. Maybe it was a Puritan guilt, nine generations of New England forebears glowering from on high, but it felt good to be busy, productive. The first frosts have flattened the garden, now scattered piles of fallen stems, dried blossoms and remembrances of an abundant summer.

Olivia invited me over for drinks one evening, with a crowd from the year-round opera staff, the singers and musicians off worldwide to their fall contracts. Wilfred, who was also invited, came in beforehand and we had some time together before going to the party. He was meeting others for dinner afterwards. The pattern of Santa Fe was resuming, small dinners with friends and an early evening drink at the artist's bar up Canyon Road.

We sat down in the studio's front room, the one with floor-to-ceiling bookshelves on either side of an old window with bubbled glass. The well-proportioned double-hung window was salvaged from the Nineteenth Century school downtown, demolished in a tasteless period for a new hotel. The old painter collected pieces before building the studio: windows, corbels from a fallen church in Nambé, doors with carved panels from Fort Marcy, and bricks from a section of sidewalk taken up for concrete replacement. A cozy room, it was perfection with the fire blazing in the corner fireplace during winter afternoons, when the setting sun filled the room with orange medallions of shimmering light from the distorted glass across the walls.

He said, "So you'll be here in the studio for a while. How does that sit with you?"

"Fine. I've figured out the kitchen, found china and silver, at least enough for breakfast every morning and a quick dinner."

"I always liked this place, almost better than your house. Maybe you should just stay on here, lease out the house, now that you don't need space for two."

"I'm thinking about that."

"You'd get a handsome rent."

"I have everything I need here. A studio, bed, a place to write, books."

"The simple life. What you've always wanted."

"Perhaps a mistake to ask for it."

"Are those Richard's ashes on the shelf up there?"

He looked up at the crowded shelves above our chairs. I had wrapped the box of his ashes, still with Barbados stamps and customs stickers, in an orange cotton cloth, one that he used to cover his Tibetan prayer cards. It sat between three volumes Dickens on the left and the teachings of the Bokar Rinpoche on the right. I had tried to change the stack of light reading on top of the box every so often, Richard always a quick study with books. Thackeray, Trollope and English mysteries.

"Yes. I piled up the volumes, to keep him amused while I was away. I sense that I need to give him a new selection, perhaps some Somerset Maugham."

"You seem better about his death, more resigned to it."

"It doesn't hurt to talk about it anymore."

"Untrammeled sex has its worth."

"It was not really all that lusty."

"Come on."

"I do believe it opened up a necessary valve. At least it appears to be open again. Curious."

Wilfred smiled as he said, "Admit it, lots of sex."

"Was it that or just getting away? I don't know."

"Take it from me."

We walked over to the house for Olivia's gathering, now a steady roar of voices over the wall. It was a strange, urban evening in my provincial house, strained laughter and an edginess in all the guests. The house was not the same with another host, awkward like a horse with a stranger's saddle.

The cosmopolitan cocktail party lived on here in Santa Fe, but it never flourished. The art community favored small dinners, brunches or picnics, but the newly arrived kept the large, stand-up and mingle cocktail party alive. Wilfred went on to his other plans when we took our exits together, and I came back to the solace of the studio.

The telephone calls to Hayden were not as fulfilling as I had expected, from the start an element of accusation, abandonment in them. My leaving was the subject we skirted around. He was pulling back into himself, not the open, sensual man that had bloomed over the summer, opening up his fragile self. The call yesterday was not different from the rest.

"Hayden, how was your day?"

"Okay, but I think I'll go to the bar for while, not really into cooking for myself."

"I wish I was there. I could take you out for the catch of the day. Our dinners together were always great. I think about them a lot."

"Me, too."

"You showed me a part that was unguarded, tender, usually over a Beef Burgundy or Chicken Paillards. I will always love you for that."

"It's not the same here without you in the front room."

"Do you still not want to come to Santa Fe? To stay with me for a while? A change of venue can make home seem better when you get back."

"Mattox, I'd hate for things to change between us. They might if I come there. Let's leave it that you'll be here next summer and we can take up from there."

"That's probably better. I miss you."

"Yeah. Also."

The distance in miles was now enlarged with distance in time when we would see each other again. The operative word was distance, more and more of it. The telephone was not an instrument that made us closer, only a reminder of how far apart we really were.

Two finished canvases sat on the studio sideboard, and a new one was on the easel with the first blocking of color almost complete. The rhythms of my studio and of home were going again; I understood my role with each. I was not sure that I understood my position with the prince of Glitter Bay, however.

The KableOne people had arrived in Santa Fe in growing numbers, renting studios for location shoots and creating excitement among the lists of young actors. My artist friends were agog, feeling important in the artificial lights and sound booms in their studios.

Brenda called me about using my studio as a location shoot for the story of the Pueblo maidens, but I told her that it was too difficult getting back to painting again to give it up just now. The hub-bub surrounding the filming was of great interest of almost everybody in town except me, what this actor said about another actor, where they would be filming tomorrow, whose house and what paintings they would include next.

I knew that my writing interest had moved on, the stories were firmly part the past. As I painted, my mind did not go the stories but to scenes from the draft novel, parts that I could rework to advantage, additions to dialogue, whole chapters that could clarify the side issues of the plot. It had become an easy, gratifying combination to think about the novel while I painted, ideas popping up like the new colors I mixed.

Brenda said, "Don't apologize. I understand about your keeping your studio closed. We're all excited about the series and think you will be once you see them on the screen."

"I know I will."

"The writers are here for only a few more days. Do you have time to meet with us?"

"How about dinner here at the studio tomorrow night? I can put together a quick meal and we can talk. I want to do everything to make the project a success."

"That sounds good."

"Six-thirty, then. Here at the studio. Olivia still has the house, so I'll do my best in the small kitchen."

"Nothing fancy. It will be good just to have the time with you."

There were more painting hours left in the morning, so I took the phone off the hook and got to work on a landscape canvas. This one was a downward focus to the foreground, no sky whatsoever, the successive rows of native shrubs, summer grasses and low ground-covers all but filling the panel, a slim suggestion of a horizon above. I had finished ink sketches of the subject a few days ago, established the back and forth patterns and the colors were fresh in my mind. If the grasses made "zees" and "exes" as they tumbled forward, the normally placid mass of leaves had an energy, an agreeable unease.

The whole afternoon as I worked at the easel I thought of Hayden, how uncomfortable he would be with this crowd of strangers coming to dinner or at Olivia's cocktail gathering the other night. He was right to be apprehensive about Santa Fe. Our dinners at the beach were personal occasions, two people who were attracted to each other, exploring the persona over plates of food. Santa Fe dinners like this one were full of difficult currents, new ideas, excitements, the very sort that Hayden felt ill at ease with.

A chicken casserole with salad (I raided Olivia's *potager* for the lettuces; after all, they were really mine) and a sliced rustic bread was what I could manage. I washed off the terrace table with a hose, brought some studio chairs to surround, and set the places with silver, napkin and wine glass. There was a knock just as I finished.

They were all there together, Brenda and the scriptwriters. They asked for glasses of red wine instead of beer; we walked through the house and settled into the studio.

Brenda said, "I wanted them to see your studio. This has what we are looking for in several of the stories, a work-place with some style, canvases arrayed about the room, one in progress on the easel, a paint table with a devil-may-care look."

Erik asked, "When do you work? Morning? Afternoon?"

"Morning usually. I try to take the phone off the hook, get three to four hours of painting done before lunch. I seldom get much painted in the afternoons."

He said, "I think of artists working in the dark hours. I read that Picasso worked at night, often all night, sleeping late. His assistants would tip-toe around the house until about noon."

I told him that I thought that was a more urban pattern, retreating into the night when the city silences began. In Santa Fe, the morning of fresh-washed sun was too fetching; it made sense to be up early at the easel, at one with the day. Most of my friends painted in the morning.

I was aware that my studio, with its perfect proportions, lent me an aura I did not have when we were all seated around a conference table. If my everyday clothes failed to bespeak the man, the studio wrapped me in impressive capes and jeweled collars. Here was the creature in his own lair, suffused in an air of creativity. It was the image that they had looked for, the surface value that Californians respected. If you had a grand studio, you must be a grand painter.

Brenda asked, "I would love to use your studio for the Cecily Brompton movie, next year. Could you spare it for a few weeks then?"

"Yes, of course. It's just too vital right now to get the patterns going again and convince the studio gods not to rebel against me."

She said, "Would Magnus Morrison have painted *plein air*? So little actually happens in that story that we wanted to get him out of his studio, along a mountain road with his folding easel. It makes a foil for the close, introspective sessions with the attractive young model."

"It was not needed in the story, but I can see the visual worth. The healthy, breezy outside contrasted with the hot sensuality of the studio."

She continued. "We have three other stories with the main characters in the country, painting. One going up around Abiquiu, and two down in the Galisteo area. The narrator in *Nature to Advantage Dressed* spends half the story there with his students and it seems to work. New Mexico has become one of our best characters."

The television series was going to be better than I had hoped. We talked through the dinner I could see that this young energy would add an excitement to my stories, transfigure them into a visual medium with ideas illustrated rather than discussed. It was the difference between talking about a painting, a piece remembered in a provincial museum, and actually seeing it. The land around Santa Fe, the mountains, the skies with banks of clouds, the red barrancas, the fields of juniper and piñon would give the stories a truth that no words could equal. No set designer could replicate the real studios of my friends, now full of lights, cables and the ever-present lens.

After the dinner guests left, I sat at the terrace table looking at the sky, finishing the last of the burgundy. It was one of those rare nights in Santa Fe when the Milky Way comes out for those willing to look up. Almost always that path of stars can be seen in Galisteo, twenty miles away, but only on a few mid-summer nights in the growing ambient light of town. I wondered if it was ever visible on the beach of Glitter Bay, did moving mean there would be no more nights like this, looking up in wonder?

If I was such an Old Person, so full of the experience of past lives, why was the future not clear? Was it at all possible to be with Hayden and make a life there, perhaps rent one of Garnet's cottages, to have dinners with Ambrose and Sylvan, afternoon teas on the beach with Garnet, long days at my writing table and bone-chilling swims in the clear pools south of Pearly Gates? I knew I could write there, but could I also paint by the sea? Would Wilfred and the others visit me there, trudging down to Garnet's for tea on the terrace, laughing at her stories? Would this sense of fullness and worth that I had brought back to life in my studio continue to grow in a beach cottage? Maybe the wisdom from the Greek cornices and Golden Rectangle would give me the answer, radiating out a glimpse of what was to come, as the cool autumn days turned into winter. A piñon fire in the corner fireplace might help.

www.ingramcontent.com/pod-product-compliance
Lightning Source LLC
Chambersburg PA
CBHW031957010726

47493CB00007B/2242